Praise for

Carol Lynne

...the start of another incredible series... The feelings between Sidney and Nash grew slowly and were wonderful to behold... I will be waiting for the next book in the Seasons of Love series. ~ *Fallen Angel Reviews*

...refreshingly unique and utterly fabulous... Interesting plot twists, engaging protagonists and strong emotion keep this engrossing novel moving at a fast pace. Ms. Lynne masterfully leaves her fans impatiently awaiting the next chapter in Nash and Sidney's captivating story. ~ *Blackraven Reviews*

There are a number of notably emotional scenes in this novel... I did find myself misty-eyed and sniffing a time or two.... Ms. Lynne leaves her readers anxious for more at the end of this novel ~ *Bookwenches*

...a lot of emotions going on in this story... Read and enjoy. You won't be disappointed. ~ *Literary Nymphs Reviews*

Books by Carol Lynne

Campus Cravings

Coach
Side-Lined
Sacking the Quarterback
Off-Season
Forbidden Freshman
Broken Pottery
In Bear's Bed
Office Advances
A Biker's Vow
Hershie's Kiss
Theron's Return
Live for Today
Incoming Freshman
A Lesson Learned
Locky in Love
The Injustice of Being
Watch Me
Coming Clean
Professor Sandwich
Big Man on Campus

Cattle Valley

All Play & No Work
Cattle Valley Mistletoe
Sweet Topping
Rough Ride
Physical Therapy
Out of the Shadow
Bad Boy Cowboy

Poker Night

Texas Hold 'Em
Slow-Play
Pocket Pair
Different Suits
Full House

Bodyguards in Love

Brier's Bargain
Seb's Surrender
I Love Rock n Roll
Taming BlackDog Four
Seducing the Sheik
To Bed a King

Dracul's Revenge

Dracul's Blood
Anarchy in Blood

Neo's Realm

Liquid Crimson
Blood Trinity
Crimson Moon
Royal Blood

Seasons of Love

Spring
Summer
Fall
Winter

C-7 Shifters

Alrik
Seger

Buck Wild

Cowboy Pride
Cowboy Rules

Lobster Cove

Welcome to Lobster Cove

Grave Diggers MC

Solo

Kings of Bedlam

The Cut

What's His Passion?

The Brick Yard

Anthologies

Naughty Nooners
Unconventional at Best
Unconventional in Atlanta
Unconventional in San Diego

Seasons of Love: Spring

ISBN # 978-1-78651-923-8

©Copyright Carol Lynne 2016

Cover Art by Posh Gosh ©Copyright 2016

Interior text design by Claire Siemaszkiewicz

Pride Publishing

Published in 2016 by Pride Publishing, Newland House, The Point, Weaver Road, Lincoln, LN6 3QN, United Kingdom.

Printed in Great Britain by Clays Ltd, St Ives plc

1

SEASONS OF LOVE: SPRING

CAROL LYNNE

Dedication

For Mark, thanks for always trying to take care of me.

Chapter One

April 1974

Ten-year-old Sidney Wilks poked a stick into the ant hill just to see the insects scatter. He dug the point of his pretend sword into one of the large-bodied ants and grinned. It wasn't a nice thing to do, but he wasn't feeling nice at the moment.

The front door opened and Sidney's father, Jackson, stepped out onto the porch. "Get out of the dirt."

"Yes, sir." Sidney stood, before brushing the dust from his pants.

"If you're gonna stay out here, sit on the porch," Jackson ordered.

"Yes, sir." Sidney sat on the end of the porch and let his feet dangle over the side. Good manners were a requirement in the Wilks' house, but inside his head Sidney was busy giving his dad a piece of his mind. Sometimes he wished a big ole bug would crawl up his dad's nose. The image almost drew a giggle from him. Almost.

If he'd had to lose a parent to cancer, why couldn't it have been his father? Yeah, it was a hateful thing to think about, but Sidney had never got on well with his dad. His mom, on the other hand, had been his entire world.

Elizabeth Running Elk-Wilks had been one of the strongest people he'd ever known. She was like a superhero. Not because she wore a cape or anything. Heck, most of the time she'd worn a big plaid shirt with a floppy leather hat she called Old Ben.

Sidney had thought his mom was indestructible. "Damn

9

cancer," he cursed. Before the ovarian cancer had ravaged her already-thin frame, taking over the rest of her body, Beth had worked right alongside the men on the Running E Ranch. She was up at four in the morning and went to bed well after Sidney. Somehow, in between, she'd managed to make her son feel like the most special boy alive.

Sidney kicked back with his heel against the lattice that surrounded the porch. Now that she was gone, he knew he'd never again be special to anyone, certainly not his father. His dad always made him feel like a disappointment. His mom had understood that he wasn't meant to be a rancher, but his father still hadn't given up hope.

It wasn't that his dad was out and out mean. He was just... hard on him. Sidney supposed his dad thought that would make him tough or something. He snorted to himself. Even at ten, he knew he'd never be like his dad.

He lay back on the porch and rested his head on his clasped hands. Staring up at the light blue painted ceiling, he wondered what the kids at school would say when he returned. His father had kept him home for the last week. There were things to be done, his dad had said. Sidney still didn't know what those things were, though. The only job he'd been given was to box up his mom's clothes. He still didn't understand why he'd had to do it so soon after her death.

Actually, now that he thought about it, Sidney was glad he'd been assigned the chore. It had given him a chance to keep a few of his mom's clothes. He hadn't kept many things, but there were a few items he'd hidden in the back of his closet.

Sidney heard the screen door slap shut and tilted his head back. He looked at Mrs O'Dwyer. She looked upside down. *Funny.*

"Sidney, wouldn't you like to have a nice plate of food?"

"No thank you, Ma'am." There were too many people in his house. They all seemed to think a piece of cake or a chicken leg would make him feel better that his mom was down in the ground. They were a bunch of buttheads.

Mrs O'Dwyer made some kind of tsking noise and returned to the house to hang out with the other adults. Sidney's dad had told him it said a lot about his mom that so many people wanted to pay their respects after the funeral. Sidney wasn't really sure what it said. Maybe the restaurants in town were closed, because everyone who came seemed to be hungry.

Sidney rolled to his side. He knew his suit was getting all dirty but he doubted he'd ever wear it again. He noticed a small bubble in the grey paint of the old floorboard. Reaching out, he ran his short fingernail over the bubble until it popped free, leaving the weathered wood exposed. He wondered how old the board was. Had his grandpa, Harry Running-Elk, built it?

"I wish you were here, Grandpa," he whispered.

A tear dripped across his nose and onto the porch. He quickly wiped his eyes with the sleeve of his coat before glancing around to make sure no one was around. There were quite a few cowboys who lived on the ranch, and the last thing Sidney wanted was for someone to tell his dad.

As he continued to pick at the paint, he remembered the whupping he'd received a few years earlier because his dad had caught him crying. Cattle on the ranch were nothing but cash crops, according to his dad. Sidney had made the mistake of developing a relationship with a calf. The little red baby's momma had refused to feed him, so it had been up to Sidney to bottle feed the little guy. His mom had warned him not to get attached to the calf, but he hadn't listened. He'd even gone as far as giving his new pet a name — Archie, after one of his favourite cartoon characters.

He still remembered running into the barn after school one day to find the special stall he'd set up empty. After searching the pasture closest to the barn with no luck, Sidney had gone in search of his mom.

At the news that his beloved Archie had been taken to the local livestock sale barn for auction, an eight-year old

Sidney had hugged his mom and broken down. It was while his mom was whispering words of support that his dad had walked into the house. He'd immediately ordered Sidney to dry his eyes and return to the barn to start his evening chores.

If only that had been all, Sidney thought, flicking flakes of paint with his finger. His dad had followed Sidney into the barn and yelled at him for being a momma's boy. He'd told Sidney real men didn't cry, especially over something as stupid as a dumb animal. It had been an hour-long lecture on what being a rancher meant. That was the moment Sidney had decided he wanted nothing to do with being a rancher.

He heard boot heels on the steps and quickly sat up, blinking away the last of his tears. Grady Nash, the newest cowboy at the ranch, walked towards Sidney. He tried to cover the damage to the porch with his hand.

Nash surprised him by sitting in the rocking chair a few feet away. "Sorry about your mom."

"Yeah, me, too." Once it was obvious Nash hadn't come to yell at him, Sidney resumed his lounging position. The bare patch of wood he'd uncovered caught his attention once more. "How old do you think these boards are?"

"No idea," Nash answered. "I reckon a lot older than either of us."

"Yeah." Sidney carefully peeled off a thick chunk of paint about the size of a quarter. He lifted it to his face and stared at it for several moments before flicking it towards the front of the porch. He wasn't sure how old Nash was, but he'd heard the cowboy tell his dad he had no plans for college so Sidney figured he was around eighteen or so.

Sidney glanced at Nash, who seemed busy making some kind of animal with his pocket knife and a piece of wood. He wondered if Nash had already eaten. Maybe he should tell him about all the food inside?

He decided against it and went back to stripping the porch. Sidney didn't see Nash talking much to people, so he figured the cowboy was a lot like him. It wasn't that Sidney didn't have anything to say, but he hadn't met anyone interested in the things he liked.

A couple of hours went by before the last of the hungry people left and the sun set over the hill. A touch to his shoulder got Sidney's attention. He rolled to his back and stared up at Nash, his gaze zeroing in on the long sideburns. Wasn't Nash too young to have that much hair on his face?

Without a word, Nash handed Sidney the piece of wood he'd spent the afternoon carving. "A deer?"

"Antelope," Nash corrected. "It's a totem. Ask your dad for a piece of sandpaper to smooth out the rough edges if you want."

Sidney pushed himself to a sitting position and ran a finger over the pointed horn of the antelope. "You know about totems?"

Nash smiled, the first since he'd come onto the porch. "When I found out your mom was Cherokee, I checked a book out of the library." He shrugged. "It interests me."

Sidney knew about them, but he'd never heard of someone's totem being an antelope. "What does it mean?" he asked, holding up the carving.

"Look it up." Nash tipped his hat and left Sidney sitting on the porch.

While staring at his totem, the porch damage caught his attention. Sidney bit his bottom lip. What had seemed like a good idea at the time had turned out to be horrible. "Dad's gonna kill me."

He was still staring at the porch when Nash's voice startled him.

"Go back inside before your dad comes out looking for you. I'll take care of this."

It was then Sidney noticed the can of paint in Nash's hand. The grey drips down the side told him Nash planned on covering up Sidney's damage. He stood and brushed his pants off, realising no amount of cleaning would help. Maybe his dad wouldn't notice? Not like he'd been out to

13

check on him in the last few hours. Sidney wondered if his dad even remembered he had a son.

Nash opened the can of paint. He used the stick Sidney had played with earlier to stir the thick grey liquid.

"Thanks, Grady," Sidney said, pocketing the totem.

"Our secret." Nash put his finger to his lips. "And call me Nash. My dad's name was Grady," he said with a tip of his hat.

Sidney smiled before walking into the quiet house. The lights in the living room were on, but no one seemed to be around. He found his dad at the kitchen table, surrounded by piles of half-eaten casseroles.

Sidney took a step back and hugged himself. It was the first time he'd seen his dad cry, and it scared him. His eyes began to burn as the intensity of his dad's sobs increased. Sidney looked around, unsure of what to do. He backed out of the room before returning to the front porch.

Nash was finishing the small painting job. He looked up when Sidney stepped onto the porch. "What's wrong?"

Sidney pointed towards the house. "My dad. He's...um." Sidney shook his head. "He's crying, and I don't know what to do."

Nash put the lid back on the paint can and rested the brush on top. "I'm sure he's just sad. Maybe he'd like a hug?"

"No," Sidney was quick to say. "He doesn't like stuff like that."

Nash stared at Sidney for several moments. "Then it's probably best to leave him alone for now. The grief process is different for everyone. Some just need to get it out all at once and be done with it."

Sidney knew Nash's dad had died the previous winter. It had even been in the newspaper. Grady Nash Sr. had been a policeman in the town of Bridgewater, only a few miles away. Deputy Nash had been trying to help a woman whose car was stuck in the snow, when another car hit a patch of ice and ran him over, killing him.

"How long does it hurt?" Sidney asked. For the first time

in a long time, he let his tears fall without wiping them away.

Nash sat on the chair he'd occupied all afternoon and pulled Sidney into his arms. "I don't know, but when I figure it out, I'll let you know."

Sidney resisted the hug at first. It felt strange for someone other than his mom to hold him like that.

"It's okay," Nash soothed, patting Sidney's back. "There's nothing wrong with crying."

Sidney relaxed slightly. "My dad doesn't like it."

"Well, your dad's dealing with his own issues right now, so this can be our secret."

With a final nod, Sidney accepted the hug. He still wasn't sure how he'd be able to live with the pain in his heart, but for the moment, it felt better.

* * * *

July 1975

With a picture of the Transamerica Pyramid building at his elbow, Sidney concentrated on the drawing in front of him. He loved the skyscrapers unique shape and wanted to see if he could duplicate it.

"Sidney!" Jackson yelled.

Sidney bowed his head. His dad hated it when Sidney spent time indoors. "Upstairs."

The sound of Jackson's boots stomping up the stairs didn't bode well for Sidney. He sat up seconds before the door opened.

"What's going on in here?" Jackson questioned.

Sidney gestured to the large sheet of paper on the floor. "I'm drawing."

Jackson took several steps forward. He stared down at Sidney and shook his head. "You've got work to do."

"I've already finished my chores," Sidney tried to explain.

"Then find more. I'm sure someone could use an extra set of hands." Jackson's gaze went to the drawing. "Where'd

15

you get that paper?"

Sidney stared up at his dad. It was obvious by the way he asked the question that he already knew the answer. "Nash bought it for me when he went into town this morning."

Jackson's hands fisted at his sides. "I don't pay Nash to shop for you."

Sidney got to his feet. In his rush to defend Nash, he forgot one of his father's most important rules. "I asked him to do it. Don't yell at him."

Jackson's eyes narrowed and Sidney knew he'd overstepped the mark. Telling instead of asking had always been a big no-no. Jackson pointed towards the bed as he unbuckled his belt. "You know what to do."

Sidney swallowed around the lump in his throat as he bent over and braced himself for the whipping that was sure to come. He opened his mouth to apologise, but he knew it wouldn't do any good.

"What've I told you about disrespect?" Jackson asked, just before the first blow landed.

The sting of the wide leather belt kept him from answering. His dad didn't want an answer anyway. He merely asked the question to justify the lashes that followed. Sidney gritted his teeth against the pain. Crying wasn't an option, according to the last lesson beat into him by his father.

Be the time the whipping ended, Sidney's butt felt like it was on fire. He took deep breaths as he attempted to stand.

From behind him, Sidney could hear the sound of his dad's belt slipping back through the loops of his Wranglers. "When's the last time you cleaned the chicken coop?" Jackson asked, before leaving the room.

"In May. Mom said in the summer..."

"Your mom's not here now. You'll listen to my rules, and I want the damn thing cleaned out at least every sixty days, you got that?"

"Yes, sir," Sidney answered. He'd read in a magazine that most people only clean their coops once or twice a year, so every two months was beyond excessive, but he kept his mouth shut.

"I'll walk you out," Jackson said.

Sidney glanced at his drawing before following his dad out of the room to the barn. He loaded the rake and shovel in the wheelbarrow before heading to the coop. With the hot July sun beating down, Sidney braced himself for the heat and smell in the small building.

Luckily, most of the chickens were keeping cool out in the yard so at least he wouldn't have to work around them. He positioned the wheelbarrow just outside the door before carrying the shovel and rake inside.

As he started to work, Sidney began to worry about Nash. Hopefully his father wouldn't yell at Nash or dock his pay for doing Sidney a favour. What if Nash got mad and refused to do anything else for him?

Movement off to his left caught Sidney's attention. Shovel in hand, Sidney turned and came face to face with the biggest snake he'd ever laid eyes on. Whether it had come in before him or after he didn't know, but the damn thing was stretched across the coop's doorway sunning itself.

Few things scared Sidney, but snakes terrified him. He looked from the snake to the shovel in his hand. The shovel's short handle would mean getting up close and personal with the six-foot long slithery beast. Sidney shivered just thinking about it. Besides, killing a rat snake would no doubt piss his dad off. Sidney thought of his sore backside.

Maybe if he waited long enough, a shadow would cast over the doorway and the snake would leave? Mind made up, Sidney rested the shovel on the ground in front of him and waited.

A while later, a sound outside the coop got Sidney's attention. *Please don't let it be my dad,* he prayed.

"Sidney?"

Nash's deep voice was a welcomed sound. "I'm in here," he called back. "There's a snake in the doorway," he warned.

Nash's handsome face appeared on the other side of the snake. He glanced from the snake with its belly still bulging from the chicken he'd obviously consumed earlier to Sidney. "How long you been in here?"

Sidney shrugged; his sweat-soaked shirt seemed to stick to his skin. "Couple hours, I guess."

Before he had a chance to say more, Nash swooped down and grabbed the snake just behind the head. "Why didn't you just kill it?" he asked, holding the long body with his other hand.

"Dad likes them. Says they keep the rats away." Sidney relaxed for the first time since he'd spotted the snake. "What'll you do with it?"

"Take it out to the brush and let it loose." Nash stared at Sidney before shaking his head. "You'd better go hose down before heat stroke sets in."

Before Nash could leave, Sidney called out. "Don't tell my dad, okay? He'd be pissed if he knew I wasn't done in here because of a snake."

Sidney couldn't read Nash's expression, but Nash eventually nodded before carrying the snake out of Sidney's sight. With a loud sigh, Sidney shook out his tense muscles before getting back to work. Once again, Nash had saved him. If Sidney was lucky, he'd still have time to finish the coop before it was time to go in and cook dinner.

* * * *

September 1977

After tossing his backpack onto the porch, Sidney headed for the barn. His first day of high school had sucked, which was nothing new. In a town the size of Bridgewater, his classmates were the same kids he'd known since kindergarten. They hadn't liked him then, and they didn't seem to like him any better after the long summer.

Before stepping into the barn, Sidney pulled his nose spray out of his front pocket. After protecting himself against the allergens in the air, he entered the dark recesses of the eighty year old barn. After his eyes had adjusted to the dim light, he grabbed the rake, shovel and wheelbarrow. Mucking out horse stalls wasn't his only chore, but it was the easiest, outside his household chores.

After his mom's death four years earlier, Sidney's dad had thrown himself into making the ranch thrive. Where his parents used to be happy making enough profit to see them through the year, Jackson Wilks now wanted more. He seemed obsessed with buying land to add to the already-large ranch.

With more land came more cows, which meant even more hired hands riding around the ranch on horses or four-wheelers. Sidney scooped up a fresh batch of horse poop and wrinkled his nose. He liked the four-wheelers better — less poop.

"How was the first day?" Nash asked, coming up behind Sidney.

Sidney dumped the shovel's contents into the wheelbarrow. "The usual." He didn't dare turn around and look at the object of his crush. It was one thing to watch Nash from the window in his room, but he didn't trust his body's response with only a few feet separating them. He squeezed his eyes shut, hoping the normally quiet man would go on about his business.

"Your dad wants me to go out to the north pasture to help one of the cows that's having trouble giving birth. Would you mind saddling Rosie for me while I gather some supplies?"

"Not a problem," he answered without turning around.

Nash's hand landed on Sidney's much smaller shoulder. "You okay?"

"Yeah. Long day."

Nash gave Sidney's shoulder a gentle squeeze before letting go. "You're on the home stretch. A few more years and you'll be able to get away from here and find your way in the world."

Sidney nodded. It couldn't happen soon enough in his opinion.

Nash's boots made a thumping noise against the floorboards as he walked towards the supply room.

Sidney took a deep breath and leaned the shovel against the wall before going to the tack room. He ran a gloved hand over the short buzz-cut his dad still insisted on. The first thing he was going to do was grow his hair out, long. Yeah, he wanted hair down to the middle of his back. He grinned to himself. Other than his light green eyes, people would have no problem noticing his Cherokee ancestry. He liked the idea of that very much.

Although his dad had always down-played Sidney's mother's heritage, Sidney had always been proud to be of Native American descent. Since receiving his antelope totem from Nash years earlier, Sidney had taken an interest in finding out more about his native culture.

After spreading the blanket on Rosie's black and white spotted back, he lifted the saddle. How many times over the years had he taken the totem out of his drawer to stare at it?

According to his research, the antelope had smarts and enough charisma to survive almost any situation. It could go a lifetime without drinking water if it needed to, instead drawing what it needed from its environment. There was a lot more to it, but those were the parts that really stuck in his head. Although why Nash thought he had charisma was beyond Sidney.

With Rosie ready to go, Sidney led the paint out of the barn. He tied her to the hitching post attached to the front of the barn. "All done," he shouted towards the supply room.

Nash came out carrying an overstuffed backpack.

"You camping out?" Sidney asked.

"Not unless I have to, but I thought it would be smart to take a bedroll and a big milk-jug of water with me just in case." Nash settled the pack onto his back before mounting Rosie.

Sidney's gaze went to the stretch of denim that covered Nash's butt. He quickly looked away before he was caught staring.

"Oh, and when you go to gather the eggs tonight, keep an eye out. I saw a big bull snake in the coop this morning, but it got away from me before I could catch it. Just don't mistake it for a rattler."

Sidney did an all-over exaggerated body shiver. He hated snakes with a passion and Nash knew it. "Are you sure you won't be back in time to gather the eggs?"

"Doubt it, but go ahead and leave them if you want, and I'll take care of them as soon as I can."

Sidney shook his head. "That's okay. I'll do it." All he needed was for his dad to find out he was shirking his chores. He watched Nash ride out before turning back towards the barn. If he hurried, he'd be able to clean the stalls and gather the eggs before dark.

* * * *

May 1982

Sidney was heading up the porch steps, royal blue graduation cap tucked under his arm, when a horn honked behind him. He turned to see Nash's dirty white pickup pull up beside the house. "Hey," Sidney greeted.

"Why'd you take off so fast? I was planning to surprise you with dinner at Charlie's." Dressed in a pair of new jeans and a nice button-down shirt, Nash looked amazing. It wasn't often Nash went without a cowboy hat, but today his hair was combed perfectly, showing off the different colours of brown to perfection.

"You were there?" Sidney asked, shocked.

"Hell yes, I was there. Couldn't have you graduate without at least someone in the crowd to whistle for you as you crossed the stage."

Sidney's brows rose. "That was you?" He'd heard the whistle but assumed it was one of the guys in his class showing his ass.

"Of course it was me." Nash gestured to the blue satin

robe draped over Sidney's shoulder. "Go toss that inside and let's go eat a steak to celebrate."

Sidney felt rooted to the spot. He'd known Nash for eight years and never had he invited him out for a meal. Was it a date? *You're such a dumbfucker,* Sidney chastised himself. He threw his hat and graduation gown onto the rocking chair beside the front door before turning back to Nash. "Okay."

Nash chuckled and shook his head as he headed back to his truck. "Good thing you're dad's not here to see that."

Although Nash was obviously talking about the haphazard way he'd rid himself of the cap and gown, Sidney felt a pang in his chest at the statement. "Yeah, guess it is," he mumbled.

"Ah, shit, I'm sorry. I shouldn't have said that." Nash slapped his forehead with the palm of his hand.

"It's okay. I know how important the cattle auction is to him." Sidney was telling the truth. He did know, he just didn't understand why an auction was more important to his dad than being at his graduation. He noticed the way Nash's hands gripped the steering wheel.

"He should've been there. An auction is no excuse in my book, but don't you dare tell him I said that." Nash turned onto the county road, heading east.

"I thought we were going to Charlie's?"

Nash grinned. "Since we're already this far out of Bridgewater, I thought we'd go on into Hutchinson. You don't mind, do you?"

"Mind? If I never go into Bridgewater again, it'd be fine with me." Sidney stared out of the window. Hutch, as everyone called it, wasn't a big city or anything but it was the closest they had without going all the way to Wichita.

Resting his forehead against the glass, Sidney wondered how often he'd come back to the ranch once he went away to college. He'd been damn lucky to get into Penn State. For the last two years he'd tried to decide on a school. His dream was to obtain a degree in Architectural Engineering and Penn State just seemed to be the right fit for him. He'd taken two years of drafting already and his high school drafting teacher had written him a glowing recommendation.

"You're quiet," Nash said.

"Just thinking." Sidney sat up and looked at Nash. "Do you think my dad would miss me if I didn't come home for breaks and stuff next year?"

Nash's lips thinned. "Honestly? I don't know, but I do know I'd miss you. You've become like a little brother to me."

Fuck! Shoot me now. "Yeah," Sidney mumbled in agreement. He had a feeling it was going to be a very long, awkward summer.

Chapter Two

December 1984

"Another week and I'll be able to buy us beer," Sidney told his roommate Josh.

"Yeah, but unfortunately you'll be back in Kansas singing Christmas carols with the other cowboys," Josh answered, offering Sidney the joint. "Want some?"

Sidney snorted and waved it away. He picked up a pack of cigarettes and shook one out. "Pass me the lighter."

Holding his breath, Josh tossed Sidney the lighter. For a straight guy, Josh had become a really good friend. The first two months of their freshman year had been a little awkward until Sidney had eventually confessed his sexual preferences. With the truth on the table, the two had built a solid friendship.

Closing his eyes, Sidney inhaled and enjoyed every second of it. He wondered how he was supposed to go without a cigarette for the entire winter break. Just imagining himself whipping out a cigarette in front of his dad after a filling dinner gave Sidney a fit of the giggles.

"Dude, what's your damage?" Josh asked, after blowing a puff of smoke out of the open dorm room window.

"Nothing." Josh's parents seemed pretty cool. No way would his roommate understand a man like Jackson Wilks. Hell, Sidney didn't even understand him.

"Hey is that guy that you told me about still there?" Josh asked.

"Nash? Yeah, Nash'll always be at the Running E." It was the only reason Sidney continued to go home. Despite all the guys he'd met and slept with since being at State, he still hadn't got over his first crush.

Sidney put out his cigarette and blew the smoke out of the window before flopping onto his bed. He gathered his hair and draped it over his shoulder, smiling to himself. It had been three years since he'd left home, three years since he'd been subjected to his dad's hair trimmer.

Although every man he'd slept with had gone on and on about his hair, Sidney doubted anyone loved it more than he did. He fingered the silky strands as he stared at the ceiling.

It had been four months since he'd seen Nash. Sidney hadn't bothered going home for Thanksgiving because he knew Nash always spent the holiday with his mom, who had moved to Phoenix after the death of her husband.

"You're pathetic," Josh said, throwing a dirty tube sock at Sidney.

"Gross." Sidney flipped the smelly sock off his chest. "What's your problem?"

"You and your five date rule."

Sidney released his hair and propped himself up on his elbows to stare at his friend. "What's the problem with my *six* date rule?"

"It's stupid," Josh said. He left his perch beside the window and fell onto his own bed. "I mean, as soon as a guy really starts to get into you, you dump him."

"I'm twenty years old. Why would I be interested in someone who's really into me? I still have five years of school left if I want my Masters." He didn't tell Josh he was secretly waiting for Nash to see him as something other than a little brother. Sidney had no use for a brother. He wanted Nash as a lover, a partner and a lifelong friend. Sleeping with others only proved that to him.

"What time does your plane leave?" Josh asked.

Sidney glanced at the clock. Was it already close to midnight? "The cab's picking me up in seven hours. Maybe I should actually pack something," he said around a chuckle. It was typical for him to arrive at the ranch with a suitcase full of dirty laundry. He glanced around the room. There were three piles of clothes — dirty, dirtier and stand-up-on-their-own gross. "What about you?"

"My brother's picking me up sometime tomorrow afternoon."

The statement drew Sidney's attention. "Luke?"

Sidney had spent the last three Thanksgiving holidays with Josh's family. He found he particularly enjoyed spending time with Josh's slightly older brother, Luke.

"Yeah." Josh began searching his drawer for something to eat. "Too bad you won't be here." Josh glanced over his shoulder and winked at Sidney. "I think he's sweet on you."

"He's gay?" Sidney really didn't have a clue.

Josh grabbed a sleeve of saltines. "Not openly, but I think he swings that way. He's always blamed sports for his lack of interest in dating, but since living with you, I've learnt the signs."

That surprised Sidney. "What signs? I give off signs?"

Josh laughed. "I'm not saying you have a big neon sign over your head that says 'QUEER'. It's just that you watch men. You don't drool over them or anything, but your attention seems to skip right over women."

"Oh." Sidney thought about it. "Yeah, you're probably right. By the way, don't use 'queer'. We like the term 'gay' better."

"Whatever," Josh said around a cracker.

Sidney ignored the roll of Josh's eyes. He wondered if Nash saw it? Although the two of them had never discussed Sidney's sexuality, he had a feeling Nash knew. He wondered if there would ever come a day when he could confess his thoughts and feelings to the one man who had always been there for him.

* * * *

Carrying Sidney's suitcase across the parking lot, Nash

kept glancing back at the younger man. Each time Sidney came home, he looked more and more different. Although Sidney had started letting his hair grow right after he'd graduated high school, the differences in his appearance on this visit were even more apparent. "You coming?"

"Yeah. Guess I should've thought to wear my sneakers instead of these boots," Sidney answered, trying to walk on the icy asphalt.

Nash stopped and waited for Sidney to catch up. "Grab hold," he instructed, offering his elbow for support.

Sidney slung the carry-on bag over his shoulder before reaching for Nash with both hands. "Thanks."

Nash readjusted his grip on the suitcase and continued towards the truck. "Not much further. Too damn many people flying in for Christmas, I reckon. I had to park in the north forty."

Sidney chuckled. "I love the way you talk. I've missed it."

"Too many fancy college fellas?" Nash asked. He was aware he wasn't as educated as the people Sidney hung around with at Penn State, but he didn't think he sounded like a hick or anything.

"Not really fancy, just different." Sidney started to chuckle when they reached Nash's truck.

"What's so funny?" Nash asked, unlocking the door. Normally he'd store the bags in the back, but with nearly twelve inches of snow in the bed, he thought better of it.

"I can't believe you're still hanging on to this old truck." Sidney climbed in and lifted his feet.

Nash put the suitcase on the floorboard before shutting the door. Getting behind the wheel, he shook his head. What had happened to the boy he'd watched grow up? "You've been here all of ten minutes, and you've already managed to insult me twice."

Sidney took off his black, pointy ankle boots before resting his feet on the suitcase. "I was not. When did you get so damn touchy?"

Nash started the truck. Was he being overly sensitive?

He glanced at Sidney. With his long hair draped over his shoulder and the black stuff lining his eyes, Sidney was both beautiful and foreign to Nash. It was almost as if Sidney wanted the world to know his sexual preference. Why now? "Buckle up."

"What?" Sidney asked. "I never wear a seatbelt."

"You will with me. They're there for a reason." Nash didn't understand folks who didn't wear them. It took two seconds to put them on.

Sidney grumbled under his breath but did as ordered.

Nash turned on the windshield wipers to sweep away the falling snow before pulling out of the parking space. Maybe if he remained quiet and concentrated on the slick roads Sidney would open up.

Over the years Nash had become accustomed to Sidney's ways, but never had he known Sidney to be intentionally hurtful. "Something bothering you?"

Sidney continued to stare out of the windshield. "Nope." There were a few moments of silence before Sidney spoke again. "Is Dad home?"

Bingo. The relationship between Sidney and his father had always been strained. From what Nash gathered, the pair hadn't got along before the death of Sidney's mom and it had only got worse over the years. Nash still didn't understand Jackson. For a father to push away any child was atrocious, but Sidney wasn't just any child. He'd been a complicated boy who had obviously longed for love and approval. How many times had Nash watched as Sidney bent over backwards to please Jackson only to be told it wasn't good enough?

After the death of his wife, Jackson had sunk into a pit of despair so deep it seemed his obsessive desire to expand the ranch was the only thing that brought him joy. Nash had considered moving on to another ranch several times, but it was his desire to give Sidney at least one person in the world who had his back that kept him at the Running E.

"Did you hear me?" Sidney asked.

Nash let the soft, unsure sound of Sidney's voice wrap around him. So young, so lost. "No, but he will be."

"Where does he go when he disappears?" Sidney asked.

"Sales, auctions. He spends a lot of time in Colorado at that feed lot he bought." Nash shrugged. "I've never pretended to understand Jackson's thinking. All I can tell you is he said he'd be home by Thursday."

"Thursday's Christmas." Sidney took a deep breath and leant his head against the back of the seat. "Fa la la la la."

Nash hadn't planned on going to the annual Bridgewater Christmas Festival, but the hurt expression on Sidney's face prompted him to at least try to make up for Jackson's shortcomings. "I don't suppose I could talk you into going to the festival with me?"

"In Bridgewater? No thanks."

"Have you ever been to one?" Nash asked. As long as he'd worked at the ranch, Nash hadn't known Sidney to go into town for the two-day event.

"Mom used to take me."

"That was a long time ago. Maybe you should give it another chance." Nash eventually made his way onto the highway, but the roads weren't much better.

"Why would I want to go? There's not a single person in Bridgewater who gives a fuck about me."

Nash opened his mouth to reprimand Sidney, but snapped his jaws shut. He had to remember that Sidney was no longer a kid. Hell, Sidney was only eight years younger than Nash. He decided to address the statement instead of the profanity. "I know the other kids gave you a hard time in school, but..."

How did he tell Sidney that he'd asked for some of the trouble he'd encountered? Nash knew from firsthand experience what it was like to grow up queer in Bridgewater. It hadn't been easy to go against his natural inclinations in order to fit in with the other kids, but it had allowed Nash a somewhat normal adolescence.

"But what?" Sidney asked, breaking into Nash's thoughts.

Since Sidney had yet to come out of the closet to Nash, it was a slippery slope. "You're not a kid anymore and neither are they. How about we both bundle up and give it a try on Wednesday?"

"Why is this so important to you?"

"I just don't want to go alone. I used to go every year with my mom and dad, but like you, we stopped going after his death." Nash glanced at Sidney. "We can't hold on to old memories forever. At some point we have to start making new ones."

Sidney squirmed in the seat, finally removing his long, black leather coat. "I could go with you."

Nash wanted to pump his fist in the air. "Good. Thanks."

* * * *

By the time Nash pulled up in front of the house, Sidney was in desperate need of a cigarette. "Thanks for coming to get me," Sidney said, slipping on his boots. He shrugged into his coat, quickly feeling the pocket to make sure he hadn't dropped his pack of smokes.

"Anytime, you know that," Nash answered. "Need help with your bags?"

Sidney opened the door. "I can get them." He climbed out and sank to mid-calf in the freshly fallen snow. He could feel the nasty stuff working its way down into his boots. *Great.* He slung the carry-on over his shoulder before grabbing the suitcase. "You're still staying in the rental, right?"

"Yeah. Good thing, too, because if this snow doesn't let up, I may be working the ranch by myself in the morning."

As much as Sidney hated the thought of helping feed the animals in the bitter cold, Nash had done more for him than anyone else in his life. "I'll help if you need me."

Nash smiled. "I may just take you up on that."

Sidney shut the door. He carried the suitcase up the drifted stairs before turning to watch Nash drive towards the tiny house he rented on the southeast corner of the ranch. The house had originally belonged to Sidney's grandfather, but after his death, Sidney's dad had started renting it out to one ranch hand or another. Nash had lived in the one bedroom house for a little over eight years, since right after his mom had moved to Arizona.

After unlocking the front door, Sidney stowed his bags in the foyer. He stood on the thick area for several moments trying to figure out where to smoke. If he went outside he'd freeze his ass off, but the thought of his dad smelling smoke in the house when he returned made Sidney cringe.

"What the hell am I worried about?" he asked himself aloud.

Sidney carried his bags upstairs to his bedroom. When was the last time his dad had ever cared enough to even step foot in his bedroom? After tossing the suitcase on the bed, Sidney crossed to the window seat. How many days had he spent, cock in hand, watching Nash work the ranch from this very vantage point?

Before lighting up, Sidney decided to dress, or in his case, undress for bed. Within moments he was naked, wrapped in a thick blanket on the window seat. "Come to papa," he said, reaching for his cigarettes and lighter.

Despite the freezing temperature outside, Sidney opened the window about six inches. He lit his first cigarette in over ten hours and inhaled, pulling all the smoke he could into his lungs. "Ahh, fuck," he moaned.

It said a lot about the quality of sex he was used to when a really good drag from a cigarette rivalled a cock deep in his ass. Sidney propped a pillow behind his back before leaning against the wall of his nook. As he enjoyed his cigarette, his thoughts strayed to Nash. No surprise there—his thoughts always ended up at Nash's front door.

Their conversation in the truck still bothered Sidney. The remark about Nash's voice had been supposed to be positive, Sidney's way of being flirty, but Nash hadn't taken it that way. The comment about Nash's truck hadn't been meant to be a slam against the cowboy either. Sidney was going to follow up the statement by asking Nash why he didn't ask for a raise. Sidney knew his father paid his ranch hands a measly amount of money, and Nash had worked too damn hard to still drive a truck he'd bought second-hand ten years earlier.

Sidney eyed the phone. He wouldn't sleep until he knew everything was okay between him and Nash. His need for Nash went far beyond anything sexual. It was the reason he'd never opened up to Nash about his sexuality. From the outside looking in, Sidney had no doubt most people would assume he was trying to replace his father with Nash, but that wasn't the case.

Nash was…sunshine. Sidney smiled at the comparison. Since the death of Sidney's mother, the handsome cowboy had been responsible for every bright spot in Sidney's life.

Sidney reached for the phone. The cord was barely long enough to stretch to the windows, but it was worth the trouble if he didn't have to put out his cigarette. It had only been twenty minutes since he was dropped off, so hopefully he'd catch Nash before he retired for the night.

"Nash."

Sidney flicked ashes out of the window. "Hey, it's me."

"Something wrong?" Nash asked.

Suddenly the cigarette in his hand felt…wrong. Sidney tossed it out of the window before answering. "I wanted to apologise for earlier. I meant it when I told you I love the way you talk. I do. There's something about your voice that seems to calm me. I didn't mean for you to think I was insulting you."

There was a long pause before Nash replied. "I guess I'm a little sensitive about it. Hell, I know I talk like a stupid cowboy."

Something in Nash's voice pained Sidney. "Don't say that. There's nothing stupid about you."

"Yeah, well…"

"I mean it, Nash. You're the best man I've ever known."

Nash chuckled. "Better stop there or my hat won't fit in

the morning."

Sidney smiled, allowing the laugh to wrap around him. "So we're good?"

"We're always good." Nash cleared his throat. "You know I'm not good with words, but I think I need to get something through that thick skull of yours."

"Thick?" Sidney asked, a grin on his face.

"Yeah, thick," Nash reiterated. "I just need you to know that I'm not going anywhere. I'll always be there for you if you need me."

Sidney's throat tightened as his eyes filled with tears. How could a good man like Nash make a statement like that when Sidney's father couldn't even be counted on to pick him up from the airport? "Can I ask you something?"

"Sure."

Sidney crossed the room to his carry-on. He dug through the black bag until he found what he was looking for. "Why? I'm nobody. We both know you could make a shitload of money working somewhere else. What is it that you see in me that I can't see in myself?" His thumb rubbed the small totem he'd been given years earlier. The horns of the antelope had been worn down to nubs, but they were still there in Sidney's mind. He was concentrating so hard on the totem that he suddenly realised Nash hadn't answered his question. "Nash, are you still there?"

Nash cleared his throat before he answered. "I'm here. Just trying to figure out a way to put my feelings into words."

Sidney closed his eyes and prayed he didn't hear the words 'little brother'. "It's okay…" he started.

"No, it's not. I should've told you a long time ago. I guess I figured you knew."

"Knew what?" Sidney asked.

"I love you. When my dad was killed, I felt lost. When I came upon you the day of your mom's funeral, I saw someone who seemed to be in the same boat. I don't know if that makes any sense, but looking after you, making sure you had someone you could count on seemed to give me a purpose."

Sidney's eyes snapped open. "Like a project?"

"No, don't think of it that way. You weren't a chicken coop that needed a new roof or a horse that needed to be rehabilitated, nothing like that. Oh, hell, I'm making a mess of this, aren't I?"

Sidney tried to focus on the positives. "So you really do love me?" Even though he knew it wasn't the same kind of love he felt for Nash, it was love nonetheless.

"Sure I do, what's not to love? Despite everything that's happened in your life, you still have a big heart. You could've easily turned into…"

"My father," Sidney said, finishing the statement.

"Yeah." Nash sighed. "If you'd just give people a chance to get close to you, I know they'd see everything I do. But you're so defensive. You purposely keep people at a distance and when you do that, you're not allowing them to see everything you are."

Sidney nodded. He knew he did that, but he didn't consider it being defensive, more like self-preservation. "In case you were wondering, I love you, too," he finally said to fill the silence.

"I know."

Sidney doubted Nash understood how much he loved him, but that was okay for now. He heard Nash yawn. "I should let you get some sleep. I just wanted to make sure you knew I wasn't trying to insult you earlier."

"I'm glad you called. See you in the morning?"

Sidney rolled his eyes. Getting up at the ass-crack of dawn to do chores didn't sound very appealing. "Sure."

* * * *

"It's freezing out here. How'd I let you talk me into this again?" Sidney asked, pulling his scarf up to cover more of his face.

Nash chuckled. They hadn't even reached Main Street

where the festival was taking place and already Sidney was bitching. "Stop complaining and I'll buy you a big cup of hot chocolate."

Nash glanced down at Sidney. With only Sidney's black-lined eyes showing, Nash knew Sidney could easily be mistaken for a woman. He prayed the townspeople didn't pay the two of them any attention.

After rounding the corner of one of the downtown buildings, Sidney moved closer to Nash. "Where'd all these people come from?"

"Good question." There appeared to be twice as many people roaming the blocked-off street as lived in the town. Nash was a loner by nature, so the crush of people combined with the bright lights and loud holiday music almost made him rethink staying.

It was the spark of amusement in Sidney's eyes that stopped Nash from turning around and heading home. "See something you like?"

Sidney pointed towards one of the food stands. Big fluffy pink and blue cotton candy hung in bags from the sides of the booth. "I haven't had cotton candy since my mom was alive."

Nash wrinkled his nose. He hated the spun sugar treat that reminded him more of insulation than candy. "Well then, let's go get you some."

Sidney smiled and took off. Nash couldn't help but grin at the younger man's enthusiasm. He followed, aware of the looks directed at Sidney as he wove through the crowd.

By the time Nash caught up, Sidney had already paid for a bag of mixed pink and blue. "I wonder if I should get two?" Sidney pushed down his scarf and opened his mouth for the first of many mouthfuls.

"Get what you want," Nash answered, putting his hand on the small of Sidney's back. Sidney nearly dropped the candy at Nash's touch, drawing Nash's attention to what he'd done. He quickly removed his hand and stuck it in his pocket. *Why'd I do that?*

Nash waited for Sidney to buy another bag of insulation before suggesting they get two big cups of hot chocolate and find a spot to watch the parade. He noticed some room along the kerb in front of the hardware store and walked that way.

Before they had a chance to sit down, a young man came out of nowhere and stood in front of Sidney. "What're you doing back here? I thought I'd seen the last of you at graduation."

Sidney took a step back, coming into contact with Nash's chest. "Sorry to disappoint you, Denny, but as much as it sucks, my family's still in Bridgewater."

Nash put a supportive hand on Sidney's shoulder. "Do you have a problem?" he asked Denny.

Denny sneered, looking from Nash's face to the hand he had on Sidney. "Looks to me like the two of you are the ones with the problem. We don't go for that queer shit here."

Nash ground his teeth but refused to move his hand. It was the kind of situation he'd tried to avoid his entire life. "We're just friends, but even if we were different it wouldn't be any of your damn business. Now I'd suggest you go on about your business and leave us to watch the parade."

Denny stuck his finger in Sidney's face. "Do yourself a favour, and stay out of town."

Nash was angered by the vehemence in Denny's voice, and started to go after him, but Sidney grabbed his arm. "Let him go," Sidney said. "I'm used to it."

For Nash it was a glimpse of what Sidney had endured growing up. How had he dealt with bullies like Denny every day at school? Nash glanced around, noticing several sets of eyes watching them. "You wanna go on home?"

"Hell, no." Sidney sat on the kerb. "You drug me to town to watch a parade, and that's exactly what I plan to do."

Nash joined Sidney. He peeled the lid off his cocoa before taking a sip. He wondered if he should let Sidney know he wasn't alone in his sexual preference. Although it wasn't the time or the place for such a conversation, Nash promised himself he'd get to it sooner rather than later.

Chapter Three

Scrawny Christmas tree in hand, Nash knocked on the ranch house door. He'd planned to get one in town, but a new round of blowing snow had made the roads impassable. Instead, he'd waded through the knee-high snow and eventually found a small cedar. The damn thing smelt a little like cat piss, but beggars couldn't be choosers.

The door opened and a sleep-tousled Sidney stared at him. Dressed only in a pair of low-riding sweat pants, it was obvious Nash had surprised him. "What're you doing out, are you nuts?"

Nash stepped to the side so Sidney could see his gift leaning against the porch column. "You can't have Christmas without a tree."

Sidney crossed his arms, hiding the majority of his lean chest from Nash's view, and stepped back to make room. "I wasn't planning on putting one up. Seems like a waste if I'm going to be here by myself."

Nash had predicted Sidney's response, which was why he was prepared. However, he hadn't predicted his reaction to the sight of the barely-clothed man. He turned slightly, hoping to hide his growing erection. *What the fuck is happening?* "Yeah, well, I'm used to having a tree. And since Jackson will be here tomorrow taking up your time, I figured the two of us could spend Christmas Eve together."

"You talked to Dad?"

"Yeah. The snow's slowed him down. The Highway Patrol closed a section of I-70, so he's spending the night in Hays. He promised to get here as soon as they get the highway ploughed and reopened."

Nash leaned the small tree against the door before pulling off his snow-covered boots and coat. The mention of Jackson had wilted Nash's cock, which was a very good thing. He'd never had that kind of reaction to Sidney. "Where can I find the stand and decorations?"

Sidney ran his hands through his long black hair, drawing Nash's attention once more. "I guess they're down in the basement."

"I'll get 'em," Nash offered.

"I'll help."

"No," Nash was quick to say. He needed a few moments to collect himself. "I'll get them if you make a pot of coffee?"

"Deal."

Nash turned on the light before making his way down the steps. The red plastic tubs were easy to spot, but he needed more time. He found an old chair and wiped it free of dust before sitting. What the hell had happened earlier? Nash shook his head, hoping to clear the image of a near-naked Sidney from his mind. *Damn.*

Nash licked his lips, remembering the sight of Sidney's thin, hairless chest and twin dark brown nipples. Why, after all the years he'd known Sidney, was he seeing him in a sexual way? It didn't make sense. Sure, Sidney was no longer a boy, but Nash was still nine years older.

It finally dawned on him why he was suddenly thinking of sex every time he looked at Sidney. Nash hadn't made his bi-weekly trip to Hutchinson to see Reece. That had to be the problem. The arrangement he had with the high school teacher was perfect for both of them. They never went out. Their strange relationship was built on sex and friendship. Period. Neither of them had the time to date or the desire to come out of the closet.

He stood and took a deep breath. God help him through the winter break. Soon Sidney would return to Pennsylvania and Nash could return to his old way of life.

Nash's gaze landed on the large oil painting of Sidney's mother stuck in the corner against the wall. He remembered a time when the painting had graced the area over the fireplace, but that had been years ago. Nash wondered if Sidney knew where it had gone. He walked over and pulled the painting out from its hiding place. Mildew had begun to grow on the canvas. Nash set it aside, along with a mental note to retrieve it as soon as Sidney returned to college.

One thing was certain, he was glad he'd insisted on coming downstairs on his own. Even the mention of Sidney's mother tended to put the younger man into a funk, and for reasons Nash refused to acknowledge, he wanted Sidney happy.

* * * *

After making the coffee, Sidney considered putting a shirt on, but the heated way Nash had looked at him earlier stopped him. For the first time, Nash had sent out signals strong enough for Sidney to pick up on. The realisation Nash was gay thrilled Sidney. Not only that, but Nash had actually looked at Sidney with a degree of desire. *Fuck.*

Hoping to elicit the same reaction, Sidney quickly ran upstairs to freshen up. As he pulled the brush through his hair, he stared at himself in the bathroom mirror. How long had he prayed for the opportunity to get closer to Nash?

The cock straining to break through the material of his old and faded sweats spurred Sidney into action. He quickly brushed his teeth before grabbing a wash cloth from the shelf. If this was to be the night, he didn't want a smelly ass to ruin the mood. Sidney ran warm water in the sink and gave himself a sponge bath.

Feeling better, he made his way back downstairs. The sad-looking tree still sat in the foyer. Sidney opened the basement door and called down, "Can't you find them?"

"Yeah, I got 'em," Nash answered.

Sidney waited for several moments, but Nash still didn't appear. "Want some help? I really am stronger than I look."

"Thanks, but after looking through the boxes, I think we just need one of them."

Sidney continued to stand in the doorway, but realised his very noticeable erection might be too threatening. He needed to play things cool. Nash obviously didn't want people to know he was gay. Sidney sent up a quick prayer. "Please, God, don't let me be wrong about him being gay."

"You say something?" Nash asked, appearing at the bottom of the steps.

"No." Sidney moved out of the way and held the door.

The scowl on Nash's face when he reached the top of the stairs wilted Sidney's erection in no time. "What's wrong?"

Nash carried the Christmas box into the living room. "Do you want to set it up in the usual place?"

"Sure." Sidney moved to clear an area, sliding the chairs out of the way and the side table into the hall. "That should work."

Nash slapped his thigh. "Dammit, I forgot the stand."

"I'll get it." Sidney was pulled up short by Nash's hand around his upper arm.

"I'll take care of it. Why don't you bring the coffee in?"

Sidney stared into Nash's eyes for several moments. It was almost as if Nash didn't want him in the basement. "What's going on?"

"Nothing. I just know where it is. It'll be quicker this way," Nash replied.

Arguing with Nash wasn't on the agenda so Sidney gave in. "Okay." He promised himself he'd sneak down later to see what Nash appeared to be hiding.

* * * *

"I used to love doing this when I was a kid," Sidney said from the living room.

Nash closed the basement door after taking down the empty tote box. Sidney was on his back under the tree, staring up through the colourfully lit branches. "Mind if I join you?" Nash asked.

It wasn't until he walked farther into the darkened room and spotted Sidney that he wished he could take back the request. All that bare skin and silky hair fanned out on the floor was too tempting, especially with the subtle twinkling lights painting a kaleidoscope of colours on the almost naked man.

Sidney lifted his head and smiled at Nash. "Only if you bring me one of those pillows off the couch."

Nash tried to think of a way to get out of joining Sidney but came up empty. He grabbed two pillows before tossing one to Sidney. Standing over the object of his attraction, Nash tried to calm his breathing. Sidney's sweats had worked their way down far enough they barely covered his cock. Nash glimpsed a teasing fringe of black hair and almost groaned.

"Aren't you coming?" Sidney asked after adjusting the pillow under his head.

"Yeah." Nash sat and positioned his own cushion about twelve inches from Sidney's. He ducked his head under the branches before stretching out. Nash wrinkled his nose. "Okay, now I can smell the pee."

Sidney laughed and playfully slapped Nash's stomach. "I told you."

"Yeah you did," he replied. Nash waited for Sidney to remove his hand but it didn't happen.

Sidney rolled to his side, putting himself even closer to Nash. "Did you ever do this when you were young?"

Nash stared into those light green eyes he'd always found so fascinating. He was being pulled in and didn't know how to fight it. "I think every kid does it."

"Really?" Sidney's hand began rubbing circles on Nash's stomach and chest. When his thumb brushed Nash's nipple through his shirt, it responded immediately. Sidney's easy-going smile turned heated. "Can I ask you something?"

No! Nash wanted to scream. Instead he said nothing. He swallowed around the lump in his throat as his cock began to fill.

"Do you like me?" Sidney asked, moving closer.

"You know I do," Nash answered, holding his ground.

Sidney's fine-boned hand travelled up Nash's neck to rest on his cheek. His bent leg moved to lie on top of Nash's, putting his groin dangerously close to Nash's thigh. "You know what I'm asking."

Yes, Nash did know. He just wasn't sure how to answer. "You're too young for me," he whispered.

Sidney's leg rubbed against the front of Nash's jeans. "I'm old enough."

Nash's chest tightened as he fought to control his desire. Sidney had given him the green light so what the hell was he waiting for? Nash rolled to his side and propped his head on his hand. "So you've already had your share of men? Because I don't want to be your first."

Sidney rimmed Nash's lips with the tip of his tongue. "You're far from the first, but why wouldn't you want to be? I thought every man dreamt of taking someone's cherry."

Capturing Sidney's tongue with his lips, Nash sucked it into his mouth. He couldn't keep his hands from roaming the slender body as he allowed Sidney to plunder his mouth. Slipping his hands between them, Nash pulled the drawstring that held Sidney's sweats in place.

Nash's touch went immediately to Sidney's tight little ass. "Oh, hell," he said, breaking the kiss.

Sidney hiked his leg higher on Nash's body, opening himself further for Nash's exploration. "Need you," Sidney said, staring into Nash's eyes. "I've always needed you." Sidney pulled back far enough to spit in his hand. He reached behind himself and coated his hole with saliva. "Touch me," he pleaded.

Nash's middle finger circled the wrinkled skin before pushing inside. The heat of Sidney's body was amazing as Nash moved the digit in and out of the smaller man's hole. He couldn't imagine what it would feel like to have his cock surrounded by such heat.

"Fuck me," Sidney said, scraping Nash's neck with his teeth. "I've dreamt of you fucking me for years."

Years? The statement pulled Nash out of the moment. He withdrew his finger and tried to move away, but Sidney continued to cling to him. "I can't do this," Nash mumbled, rolling to his back.

Sidney's hand cupped Nash's erection. "Don't worry. I'll talk you through it."

It dawned on Nash that Sidney had misinterpreted his statement. He reached down and stilled Sidney's hand when he started to unzip Nash's jeans. "No. I know very well how to fuck a man."

"Mmmm, I bet you do." Sidney kicked his sweats off before trying to climb on top of Nash.

"This isn't a good idea," Nash protested. "Not only don't we have stuff, but you're leaving in another week and a half."

"I have lube and condoms up in my bag." Sidney started to get up, but Nash held him in place.

Nash closed his eyes and hugged Sidney against his chest. It would be so easy to just let go and enjoy everything Sidney had to offer, but where would that leave them? What happened when Sidney returned to college? Nash had no doubt he'd easily slip into the jealous lover role. Imagining Sidney off at school with an entire campus of men to cruise didn't sit well at all. Besides, he loved Sidney. What would happen if the two of them had a lover's quarrel and never spoke again? Not only would Nash be out of a job, but he'd break the promise he'd made years earlier always to be there for Sidney.

"Fuck!" Nash rolled Sidney off him and rose up on one arm. Staring down into those gorgeous green eyes, Nash hated what he was about to say. "I can't fuck you once and forget it."

"So don't forget it."

Nash didn't miss the hurt expression on Sidney's face when he said it. "I need you in my life, but as a friend. If we

44

bring sex into it, nothing between us will ever be the same."

"I know," Sidney agreed. "Things can be so much better between us."

Nash shook his head. "Or worse, and I won't risk losing you for a fuck."

Sidney grabbed his sweats before turning away from Nash. He scooted out from under the tree and stood. "Guess I didn't realise that's all it would be to you."

The thick emotion in Sidney's response worried Nash. Hurting the younger man was what he was trying to prevent. "Sidney," he called, holding his hand out in the retreating man's direction when he noticed the tears running down Sidney's face.

"Lock up when you leave," Sidney said before running up the steps.

Nash heard Sidney's door slam shut. "Fuck."

He knew he shouldn't, but Nash couldn't help himself. Leaving Sidney on Christmas Eve with that sad look in his eyes would haunt him far beyond the holiday season. He climbed the stairs, hoping he wasn't making the biggest mistake of his life.

"Sidney?" he called, knocking on the closed door.

When he received no answer, he tried the knob and found it to be unlocked. Stepping into the room, Nash took a deep breath. "I'm sorry." Nash went to sit beside Sidney on the bed. "I was wrong to say what I did. There's no way in the world making love to you would be just another fuck. Maybe that's what scares me the most."

Dressed only in the pair of sweats, Sidney swivelled around to face Nash. "I know what it feels like to be fucked. But just once I wanted to know what it felt like with someone who genuinely cared for me."

Nash couldn't argue the point. He wanted the same thing. "Come here," he said, opening his arms.

When Sidney moved into his embrace, Nash crushed the younger man against his chest. He buried his face in the long black hair he loved to touch. They may only have one night together, and Nash was still worried it would be a huge mistake, but he couldn't deny himself or Sidney the experience. He cupped Sidney's cheek before delving in for another kiss like the ones they'd shared downstairs. As he plundered Sidney's mouth with his tongue, Nash reached between them and unbuttoned his shirt. He wanted to feel Sidney skin-to-skin.

Sidney wasted no time taking over for Nash. He pushed the shirt from Nash's shoulders before breaking the kiss. Sidney licked his way down Nash's neck, across his collarbone and down to his chest. He attached his mouth to Nash's nipple and sucked, drawing moans of pleasure from Nash.

Nash buried his fingers in the back of Sidney's hair and held him in place as he lay on the bed. "Feels good."

"Mmm hmm," Sidney answered, without taking his mouth from Nash's pebbled nub.

The attention was having a direct effect on Nash's cock, which swelled to press against the zipper of his jeans. He pulled Sidney on top of him, needing the pressure Sidney's body provided. God, if Sidney's mouth felt so good on his chest, what would those lips feel like surrounding his cock?

As if reading Nash's thoughts, Sidney released Nash's nipple. "Want to taste you."

Nash nodded, thrusting up against Sidney in a silent plea.

With a wide grin on his gorgeous face, Sidney scooted down until he was insinuated between Nash's spread thighs. Sidney ran his hand over the obvious erection still trapped inside Nash's jeans. He followed the touch with his mouth, scraping the faded denim with his teeth.

Nash groaned. "Take it out before I explode in my underwear."

Sidney popped the button before slowly lowering Nash's zipper. "I can't believe I'm about to do this."

Neither could Nash, but there was no way in hell he could call a halt to it. He reached down and pushed his jeans and underwear down far enough for his cock to spring free. He'd have preferred to remove them completely, but dislodging Sidney from between his legs wasn't something Nash wanted either.

The first touch of Sidney's tongue to the tip of Nash's cock almost set him off. Nash fought for control, hoping to stave off his climax until he had a chance to make love to Sidney. "Don't tease. I'm too damn close."

After gathering a large drop of pre cum on his tongue, Sidney crawled up the length of Nash's body for a deep kiss. Nash moaned at the combined taste as he tried to get both of them undressed. He needed to be inside Sidney's heated body. Just once, he wanted to show Sidney without words how much he loved him.

Using his own pre cum for lube, Nash separated Sidney's ass cheeks. He delighted at the funny noises Sidney made when Nash breached Sidney's hole with his finger.

"Lube," Nash said, after a few pumps of his hand.

Sidney rose up and looked down with a gaze so sultry it nearly fried Nash's brain. "I'll get the lube, but I prefer you go easy on it," Sidney practically purred.

Nash swallowed. Was it possible Sidney's sexual experiences outweighed his? Nash let out a slow breath when Sidney crawled off him and walked across the room, comfortable in his nudity. Nash had always been a fairly confident lover, but there was something about Sidney that gave him pause. What if he didn't measure up?

Sidney reached into his bag and came out with a tiny, well-used bottle of lube. He clutched it in his hand. "Promise me you'll only use enough to get inside?"

Nash rolled to one side of the large bed, as nervous as a virgin. "Okay." Evidently Sidney enjoyed a bite of pain, and although Nash wasn't used to it, he wasn't completely against it. The whole idea was to give Sidney a night he wouldn't soon forget, right?

Nash marvelled at Sidney's smile as he climbed back onto the bed. It was nice to see the man look truly happy for a change. Nash held out his hand, and Sidney passed him the lube.

"Don't worry, I'm used to it." Sidney turned a deep shade of red. "That came out wrong. I don't want you to think I…"

"I don't," Nash said, cutting Sidney off. He didn't want to think of all the men who'd fucked Sidney. Although Nash had never been fucked without lube, he had been fingered with nothing but spit and it burned like hell. "Can I ask you something?"

"Sure." Sidney settled beside Nash. He rolled to his side and draped an arm over Nash's chest.

"Do you want me to hurt you? Is that it?" Nash asked.

Sidney's hand began to rub across Nash's lightly-haired chest before moving down to tickle the short pubes surrounding Nash's cock. "No, it's not that, but I've found I don't enjoy being fucked as much when things are too slick down there. I want to feel everything with you. I'm not completely naïve. I know I'll be sore for the next couple days, but that's what I want." Sidney leant over Nash and kissed him. "I want a reminder of this night."

Nash dived in for another kiss. He swept his tongue around the interior of Sidney's mouth as he came up with a plan. No lube. Spit would have to work. Although Nash had never rimmed a lover, the idea of doing it to Sidney appealed to him. He broke the kiss. "Roll over."

With a cute little giggle that made Nash's stomach quiver, Sidney flopped onto his stomach. Sidney smiled at Nash as he slowly spread his legs apart and pulled his knees under him.

Fuck. It was the first good look Nash had been given at Sidney's beautiful ass. "Perfection," he whispered to himself.

Sidney laughed. "I wouldn't go that far."

"I would." Nash moved to kneel behind Sidney. Suddenly the thought of rimming the perfect asshole with his tongue didn't bother him at all. Separating Sidney's ass with his hands, Nash leant in and swiped the flat of his tongue over the wrinkled skin.

Whether it was the texture against his tongue or Sidney's reaction to it, Nash didn't know, but he moaned and continued to give the dark-skinned pucker a thorough tongue bath.

"Jesus!" Sidney cried. "Fuck me. Please," he begged.

Nash applied more spit to the relaxing hole before inserting a finger. Sidney's body accepted the intrusion easily, prompting Nash to add a second finger. It didn't take long before Sidney started fucking himself on Nash's fingers.

"Now," Sidney moaned.

Nash reached for the lube. As promised, he used only a drop or two to coat his cock. "Ready?"

"Hell yes."

Holding his cock by the base, Nash pressed the crown to Sidney's hole. He applied pressure, but waited for Sidney's body to accept the thick head. With another groan from Sidney, Nash pushed his crown past the outer ring of muscles. Sidney had been right — fucking without as much lube certainly did slow the process down.

"Yessss," Sidney hissed. "More."

Nash rocked his hips back and forth until his entire length was buried deep inside Sidney's ass. He let out the breath he hadn't realised he'd been holding. "Tell me when you're ready."

"Don't wait for me," Sidney answered through clenched teeth. "Do it."

"Not going to hurt you," Nash replied, although his body was beginning to have other ideas.

"You won't." Sidney began to move, fucking himself.

Relenting, Nash gripped Sidney's hips and began a slow, but hard, rhythm. What had he ever done in his life to deserve such a perfect moment? His body was on fire while his soul soared high above them both.

Sidney moved one hand under himself before looking over his shoulder at Nash. "Squeeze my balls. Hard."

Yet another request Nash had never heard uttered by a lover. He reached down to find the perfectly shaped orbs and did as instructed.

"Harder. I need to come," Sidney panted.

Sweat dripped down the side of Nash's face and he used his free hand to wipe it away. He applied more pressure to the precious sac hanging under Sidney. It had to have been painful, but Sidney moaned louder at the tightening of Nash's grip.

"Coming," Sidney warned, seconds before his body jerked with his climax.

Nash released Sidney's testicles. He returned his attention to fucking Sidney as hard as he could. It might be different for Nash, but Sidney obviously enjoyed the rough play. It wasn't long before Nash could feel his own impending orgasm. "Gonna," he grunted.

As his climax raced through him, the individual hairs on Nash's body stood on end. He rested his forehead on Sidney's spine as he rode out the last of the explosion.

Sidney collapsed to the bed with Nash on top of him. "Fucking perfect," he mumbled.

Unable to talk, Nash nodded and wrapped his arms around Sidney. It took a few moments for his head to clear, but soon Nash began to wonder what he'd just done. He'd been worried about the emotional impact of fucking Sidney, but he hadn't counted on the physical impact. After one night with the younger man, Nash knew he'd never be sexually satisfied with anyone else. Was it possible to become addicted to something after only sampling it once? Shit!

Nash withdrew despite Sidney's vocal protest. He needed a moment to process everything that had just happened. He rose off the bed. "Be right back."

He used the need to pee as an excuse to escape into the nearby bathroom. After turning on the faucet, Nash splashed cold water on his face before grabbing a washcloth. He continued to use the cold water to clean his cock in the hope his newfound addiction to Sidney's body would cool.

Nash knew he had two choices, go back into the bedroom and climb under the covers, or run away from Sidney as fast as he could. It was no longer a question of whether he would be jealous after Sidney left, but how much it would affect the rest of his life.

He moved to turn the tap to warm before rinsing out the washcloth. With a heavy heart, Nash carried the cloth into the bedroom and set it on the bedside table. Sidney was already under the covers but still awake.

"I should get out of here," Nash said.

"Stay with me."

Nash shook his head. "Neither of us knows what ungodly hour Jackson might pull up. And if I lay down, I'll be sound asleep within seconds." He retrieved his clothes from the floor. He longed to tell Sidney how much their love-making had meant, but hated to give the younger man false hope. Nash dressed quickly before bending over to place a soft kiss on Sidney's lips. "Merry Christmas."

"Merry Christmas," Sidney mumbled. It was apparent Sidney was bothered by Nash's impending departure.

Nash smoothed Sidney's hair away from his face. Sidney would never know how hard it was for him to leave, but Nash knew he had no choice. He gave Sidney one last kiss before walking out the door.

Before he left the house, Nash unplugged the Christmas tree lights.

After turning off the rest of the downstairs lights, he stood at the bottom of the staircase for several long moments. If there was even the slightest chance that something could work out between the two of them, he'd put his fears aside and run up those stairs, but he knew the truth. Sidney's life was in the city. Not much call for architectural engineers in farm and ranch country. Especially not for a man like Sidney who had always wanted to design high rise buildings and museums.

Nash briefly thought about moving to the city and snorted.

Talk about a duck out of water. Other than the poor beasts being made to pull fat tourists around parks, there weren't many horses in the city.

He crossed the foyer and lifted his coat off the peg beside the front door. Pulling out a small wrapped present, Nash shook his head. He should've given it to Sidney earlier in the night before he'd let things go too far between them. Nash carried the gift into the darkened living room and set it under the tree. At least Sidney would have one present to open.

* * * *

On Christmas morning, Sidney woke to the sound of a diesel truck right outside his bedroom window. He didn't need to get up to know his dad was home. Staring at the ceiling, Sidney knew why he wasn't jumping out of bed. He turned over and pulled the covers up around his neck.

"Sidney!" Jackson yelled from the bottom of the staircase. "Get up. I need your help."

Sidney squeezed his eyes shut. Maybe if he pretended to be asleep his dad would go about his business.

The bedroom door opened before Sidney had a chance to put on his sleeping face. "I need help unloading a horse I brought back for Nash."

It was the mention of Nash's name that finally got Sidney's attention. "Nash already has a horse."

"Not like this one. Get up."

With a groan of protest, Sidney sat up. "Give me a few minutes to wash my face and put on some clothes."

Jackson's head tilted to the side as he stared at Sidney. "Yeah, you'd better wash all that shit off your eyes unless you want someone to mistake you for a woman."

Sidney rubbed the skin under his eye and came back with a black smudge. He usually made a habit of washing his face before bed, but the situation with Nash the previous night had left him in tears. Although Nash hadn't said it,

Sidney knew it was their one and only night together.

When it didn't appear his dad was in a hurry to leave, Sidney gestured to his nude chest. "You mind?"

"Oh," Jackson said. "I'll meet you in front of the barn."

Sidney waited until the door closed before throwing the covers off his naked body. The thought of going out in the bitter cold on Christmas morning turned his mood from grumpy and sleepy to bitchy in a heartbeat. His dad hadn't even bothered saying 'Merry Christmas', the bastard.

Although his ass was as sore as he'd expected, it hadn't left Sidney with the euphoric feeling he'd hoped for. He dressed quickly before pulling his hair back into a loose ponytail. Sidney knew his hair drove his dad crazy, and if he were completely honest with himself, he'd admit it was the main reason he'd grown it out. Of course it wasn't the only reason. Other men seemed to really love it. How many times had a man buried his face in the back of Sidney's neck while fucking him? They all commented on the citrus scent of his shampoo and how soft the long strands felt against their skin.

"Today, Sidney!" Jackson yelled.

Sidney made a face before opening the door. At least he doubted his dad would be home for more than a few days. His dad hadn't been around for Sidney's birthday for years, why change the routine now?

By the time Sidney had pulled his boots on and shrugged into his coat, hat and gloves, his dad was already outside honking the horn. "I'm coming!" he yelled, stepping out onto the front porch.

The man had to be a complete idiot to drive a horse trailer from Colorado to Bridgewater during a blizzard. Sidney joined his dad at the back of the trailer. Never had he been asked to unload cattle or horses, so the request still bothered him. "What's so special about this horse that you want my help?"

The horse chose that moment to kick out with his back leg, striking the trailer door. Jackson glanced from the horse to Sidney. "Diablo has issues."

Sidney moved around to the front of the trailer so he could better see the black horse's face. "What the hell happened to him?"

The word was out before Sidney had a chance to take it back. The fist that punched him in the side of the face was a good reminder of what not to say around his father. Because of the slippery ice and snow, Sidney lost his balance and fell to the ground. He raised his arm to ward off any further blows. "Sorry, Dad."

Jackson grunted. "Just because you're off at school doesn't mean you can forget the rules of the house."

"I know." Sidney waited for permission to get up. As he continued to lie there, his body heat began to melt the snow under him, soaking his jeans to the skin.

"Go get one of those feed sacks to put over Diablo's eyes while we try to get him out of the trailer in one piece," Jackson ordered.

Sidney wasn't worried about the horse as much as he was concerned for his own safety at the hands of his father. Jackson rarely struck Sidney, but when he did his mood generally lasted for hours, sometimes days.

Sidney scrambled to his feet. He didn't dare look at his dad before rushing into the barn for the sack. It took him several moments to find one that looked clean enough to risk putting over Diablo's eyes and when he returned to the trailer, Sidney could tell his dad was quickly losing patience. "Sorry."

Jackson moved with precision to get the horse haltered. He tucked the feed sack around the halter, but not before Sidney got a good look at the horse's scarred head. Once again he wondered what had happened to the poor animal.

"Okay, now come up here and hold tight to the harness while I open the door."

Diablo was starting to get restless again. The moment Jackson released his hold, and before Sidney could get a good grip on the harness, the horse jerked his head back and kicked the door once again.

"God dammit, Sidney! Hold him still!" Jackson yelled.

Sidney was grateful his father wasn't within striking distance. As it was, Sidney was going to have to lie to Nash about the blossoming bruise he could feel rising on his face. Only once before had Nash seen Jackson's handiwork and it hadn't been pretty. Usually his dad had better control over himself and if he did direct his anger at Sidney it was usually in a place that wasn't visible.

However, several years ago, Jackson had made the mistake of blacking Sidney's eye in a fit of anger. Nash had seen Sidney when he'd dropped by the house unexpectedly, and it had taken Sidney an hour to calm Nash down. The last thing Sidney wanted was for Nash to give Jackson what he deserved and get fired as a result. Sidney needed Nash too much to risk it. Nope, he'd tell Nash he'd obtained the bruise wrestling to get the horse out of the trailer.

The trailer door opened, and Diablo nearly jerked Sidney's arm out of its socket in his haste to free himself. "Steady, boy." Sidney tried to soothe the horse but with Jackson's heavy hand on the lead affixed to the harness, Sidney's gentler treatment went unnoticed by Diablo.

Knowing it would get him into trouble, but unable to hold on, Sidney released the harness. "I don't have hold of him anymore," he shouted to his dad.

Sidney jumped off the side step of the trailer and ran around to the back in case he was needed. "Should I get another rope?"

"Open the corral gate," Jackson ordered.

"I thought you were planning to put him in the barn?"

"Don't argue with me!" Jackson screamed.

Sidney bit his tongue and raced towards the wide corral gate. Once he'd swung it open, he understood what his dad was trying to do. The gate hit the edge of the trailer, blocking Diablo's escape on that side. Sidney felt stupid for not realising it. No wonder his dad hated it when he questioned him.

Jackson worked alone for several moments before yelling at Sidney once again. "Don't just stand there, get your butt back over here and guard this other side."

Sidney made sure the gate wasn't going anywhere before running back around the trailer and pickup to stand on the left side of the trailer as Jackson tried to control the thrashing horse.

As if in slow motion, Diablo span towards Sidney and reared up on his hind legs. The giant hooves came within inches of smashing Sidney's face in. Out of nowhere, two strong arms shoved Sidney out of the way.

Sidney fell to the ground as Nash reached up and grabbed Diablo by the harness, giving the horse a good yank. The horse's hooves returned to the deep snow. Nash got right in Diablo's face and ripped off the grain sack.

Man and horse stared at each other for several moments before Nash spoke. "You okay, Sidney?"

"Yeah," Sidney answered, glancing at his dad.

He could tell by his dad's red-faced expression that he wasn't happy about the events that had just taken place. "Get him in the barn," he told Nash.

Nash broke eye contact with the horse and stared at Jackson. "You should've called me. Do you have any idea how close you just came to losing your son?"

Jackson handed the lead to Nash. "Maybe if he'd paid a little more attention over the years, he'd have been better equipped to handle the situation."

Still on the ground, Sidney was frozen in place by the skill with which Nash handled the horse. As Nash led the stallion into the barn, Sidney couldn't help but notice the scars on the horse. There was no doubt Diablo had once been a beauty and although Sidney didn't know everything there was to know about ranching, he could damn well tell an expensive animal when he saw one.

"Merry Christmas," Jackson grumbled, entering the barn.

Sidney took the opportunity to get to his feet. He brushed himself off before stepping just inside the open barn door.

"What happened to him?" Nash asked, easing Diablo into the stall on the end.

"What's it look like?" Jackson asked.

"Looks to me like someone took a whip to him, but I can't rightly figure out why someone would do something so cruel," Nash answered.

"Diablo has the bloodline to be a champion in the ring, but he's a stubborn, mean son-of-a-bitch. A friend of mine's son took the whip to him in an effort to get him under control, but it only made Diablo's temperament worse."

"Well, no shit," Nash mumbled so softly Sidney barely heard him. "So why bring him here?"

"I told my friend if anyone could get through to that horse it'd be you," Jackson informed Nash.

Nash filled the water bucket before breaking off a flake of hay and settling it in Diablo's feeder. After the horse was taken care of, Nash locked the stall. He turned back to Jackson. "If I'm to work with him, you have to give me your word no one else will mess with him."

"All right," Jackson agreed.

Sidney was fascinated by the entire situation. Why would his father allow Nash to speak to him the way he did? Sidney knew Nash had been acting as the foreman when Jackson was away from the ranch—did that have something to do with it? Just how often was his dad away?

Nash made a detour around Jackson and came to stand in front of Sidney. He tilted Sidney's face to the side. With narrowed eyes, he brushed the tender skin of Sidney's face with his callused thumb.

"How'd this happen?" Nash asked.

Lying to Nash wasn't something Sidney could bring himself to do, especially after what they'd shared the night before. "It's Christmas," he finally whispered. "Let's just enjoy the day."

Sidney watched as Nash's jaw clenched. It was obvious there was a war going on inside the older man. Sidney glanced at his father who was watching the play between

Nash and his son closely.

"Don't get yourself fired," Sidney told Nash. "Please."

"Will you be okay alone with him today? Because I'm afraid of what might happen if I stick around."

Sidney nodded. "I'm okay."

Nash released Sidney's chin and stepped back. "Why don't the two of you go on in the house and get some dry clothes on? I'll put away the truck and the trailer."

"I'm making ham for dinner. You're welcome to come," Sidney offered.

"Maybe another time. I've got chores to do and a new stallion to figure out." Nash physically turned Sidney around to face the barn door. "Go on to the house before you catch pneumonia."

Sidney did as he was told, but Christmas had already lost its appeal. With any luck, his dad would head back to Colorado soon, and he'd be given the opportunity to learn what that look in Nash's eyes meant.

Chapter Four

After breakfast, Jackson went up to take a shower while Sidney did the dishes. As he scrubbed the cast iron skillet with hot water and a lot of elbow grease, Sidney watched Nash out of the window. The easy manner in which Nash moved awed Sidney. Even the single digit temperatures outside didn't seem to bother Nash as he methodically fed the cattle, his cowboy hat pulled down to help shield his face from the blowing snow.

Sidney set the skillet on the stove before turning on the burner. Breakfast had been a silent affair. He hadn't missed the glances aimed his way by his dad. Sidney wondered if it was the bruise that had blossomed on his cheek or the eye liner he'd put on after his hot shower.

It was obvious Jackson hated his only son wearing makeup, but so far Sidney hadn't been yelled at for it. Of course the day had barely started and after the smack-down outside, his dad seemed to be on his best behaviour.

The smell of the hot cast iron reminded Sidney to turn off the burner. He crossed back to the window to get another look at Nash. He couldn't help but smile as Nash walked behind the snow blower. Damn, he loved a pair of bowed legs.

"I'm going to lie down for a while," Jackson yelled down the staircase.

"Okay," Sidney answered. He waited until he heard his dad's door shut before putting on his coat and boots. He checked his pocket to make sure his cigarettes hadn't fallen out in the earlier foray into the bitter cold before opening the front door. He walked to the end of the porch, out of

59

Nash's view, and lit up.

One thing was for certain, standing out in the frigid temperatures certainly cut down on his desire to smoke. He stared at the Christmas tree through the window. Although he hadn't got around to turning the lights on, the tree itself served as a reminder of the previous night's events.

His initial reaction was to smile as he remembered the feel of Nash touching him, fucking him. After Nash had gone home, Sidney had had a chance to really think. Nash hadn't said he didn't want to be with Sidney again, but he had a strange feeling it was a onetime deal with Nash. Maybe if Sidney opened up and told the older man how he felt, Nash would change his mind.

Sidney inhaled once more on his cigarette before dropping it off the end of the porch into a snow drift. He'd eventually have to come out and gather up his butts, but he felt certain his secret was safe for the moment.

A huge part of him wanted to run out to the barn and throw himself into Nash's arms. Confession was good for the soul. Wasn't that the saying? Sidney shrugged. Before he could do anything, he needed to brush his teeth and wash his hands or else he and Nash would never get around to being honest with each other.

After washing up, Sidney picked up the envelope from his dresser. He wished his gift had been finished before Christmas, but hopefully Nash would feel it was worth the wait.

Before leaving the house, Sidney stopped by the living room and plugged in the tree. A small wrapped package caught his attention. Sidney set Nash's envelope aside before picking up the gift. "To Sidney From Nash."

Sidney hugged the present to his chest before opening it. His heart warmed at the hand-carved totem pole. Although miniature in size, the totem included six different animals. Sidney couldn't help but wonder what it meant. It had to mean something. Nash never gave a gift without meaning behind it.

It was the perfect excuse to seek Nash out in the barn. With the totem tucked inside his jacket, Sidney picked up the envelope and headed outside.

He waved to Nash, who was spearing another big, round bale of hay with the tractor, and pointed towards the barn. While he waited for Nash, Sidney tried to get a better look at Diablo. After Nash's warning earlier, Sidney didn't dare get close to the stall. Instead he just studied the horse from where he was. "Sorry that happened to you, boy," he told the horse.

The door opened and a blast of cold air hit Sidney. "Everything okay?" Nash asked.

"Yeah." Sidney unzipped his coat before pulling out the totem. "I wanted to thank you for your gift."

"You're welcome." Nash nudged his cowboy hat up, giving Sidney a better view of Nash's eyes.

"Can I ask you a question about it?"

"Sure." Nash took off his gloves before using them to knock the snow from his coveralls.

"I thought I reminded you of an antelope, so what're all these other animals for?" Sidney asked, running his fingers over the carvings.

"I think you're in transition right now. You share characteristics with each of those animals. Which one will end up being your true totem we'll have to wait and see."

Sidney knew better than to ask what the different animals meant. He'd look it up in the book he'd bought once he returned to school. "Anyway, I wanted to tell you how much I love it." He looked up into Nash's big, brown eyes. "I got you something, but it's not done yet, so you'll have to settle for a crappy card."

Nash grinned. "Nothing given from the heart is crap. Remember that."

Sidney shuffled his feet and held out the envelope. He waited for Nash to open it. The card was just a generic, run-of-the-mill Christmas sentiment, but inside was a copy of a picture he'd drawn up.

"I love it," Nash said, after unfolding the sheet of paper.

Sidney chuckled. "The picture isn't your present. I'm having a pair of chaps made for you. I found this old guy on the internet that makes them customised. Unfortunately, the guy's older than I thought and it seems to be taking him a lot longer than I'd hoped."

Sidney pointed to the drawing. "Anyway, he's going to put your name on them in a lighter shade of leather. I put the star on there in memory of your dad with his initials in the centre, hope that's okay."

Nash folded the drawing before sticking it back into the envelope. "I've never had a pair of chaps," he said in a soft voice.

Sidney's gut clenched. Did that mean he didn't want them? "I can probably try to cancel them if you'd rather have something else?"

Nash glanced up from the envelope with a hint of moisture in his eyes. "No. This is the best gift I've ever been given." He reached out and pulled Sidney into his arms. "Thank you."

"You're welcome." Sidney wished Nash wasn't so bundled up. He would've loved to kiss the area of skin just above Nash's shirt collar.

"I'm sorry if I hurt you last night," Nash said. "Believe me, if I thought we had a future, I'd take you back to bed for the rest of the winter."

Tilting his head back, Sidney kissed Nash's stubbled chin. "So you don't sleep with people unless there's a future in it?"

"I didn't say that." Nash kissed Sidney's forehead. "But I won't sleep with you again without it. You mean more to me than a friend with benefits type of arrangement."

There was something in the way Nash said it that made Sidney curious. Nash had to be getting sex somewhere, but where? "Who do you fuck?"

Nash's eyebrows rose at the frankness of the question. "A teacher from Hutchinson. We try to meet up every couple of weeks."

Although Sidney had gone to bed with a number of guys over the previous three years, knowing Nash had someone hurt. "What's his name?"

"Reece Lyons." Nash brushed a stray lock of hair out of Sidney's face. "The situation works for us because he can't come out, and I've no reason to."

Sidney swallowed around the lump in his throat. "How long?"

"A while."

It was obvious Nash didn't want to go into further details about his arrangement with Reece, but Sidney knew it would continue to pick at him. He hated the thought of someone else getting what he craved.

"Is this Reece guy the reason you won't sleep with me again?"

"No. I've already told you my reasons. You're not Reece, Bob or Tim. You're Sidney. My Sidney. And I won't risk either of us getting more hurt than we'll already be when you leave."

Sidney sighed. "You know that doesn't make sense, right?"

"It makes perfect sense to me. My life is here, yours isn't. But I couldn't stay at the Running E if something happened to break up our relationship." Nash kissed Sidney's forehead again. "You mean too damn much to me."

Sidney wanted to argue that they belonged together, but he knew Nash was right. Sidney didn't belong in Bridgewater and he couldn't imagine Nash anywhere else. Would he be destined to live the life of a slut, just going from bed to bed? Because he knew in his heart no other man would live up to Nash. A touch to his bruised cheek brought Sidney out of his thoughts.

"You going to tell me how this happened?" Nash asked, examining the bruise.

"It was as much my fault as his. I made the mistake of cussing within arm's length."

"Dammit," Nash spat. "I told him last time what would happen to him if he ever laid a heavy hand on you."

Sidney leant in to Nash's touch. He was grateful Nash didn't know about the other times. It wasn't that his dad was a big bad abuser or anything. Jackson just had a short fuse and Sidney seemed to set him off more often than not. "Like I said, I knew better than to cuss in front of him, so I'm as much to blame."

"Bullshit. Breaking rules is grounds for punishment, but I wouldn't call that bruise on your face a proper punishment." Nash tapped Sidney's nose. "What do you think he'll do if he catches you smoking?"

The question surprised Sidney. "You know?"

Nash chuckled. "Of course I know. I honestly doubt there's much about you that I don't know."

"Such as?" Sidney asked, curious.

"I know you wear your mom's pink cardigan when you're sad," Nash began.

"How?" Sidney was mortified.

"I've seen you sitting in the window, wrapped in that ugly thing more times than I care to count. It usually follows a fight between you and Jackson, so I figure the sweater makes you feel better."

"It does," Sidney confessed. "Although it doesn't smell like my mom anymore."

"White Shoulders," Nash said.

"Huh?"

"Your mom smelled like White Shoulders. It's a perfume. Buy yourself a bottle and spray some on her sweater."

Sidney's head tilted to the side. "How do you know what perfume she wore?"

Nash shrugged. "I may not have known her for long, but I knew her. My grandma used to wear the same perfume, that's how I know the name."

White Shoulders. Sidney made a mental note to pick up a bottle once he returned to school. Shit, that wouldn't work. As much as he loved his mom's things, he'd never take them to school. Josh would have a field day if he found perfume in Sidney's sock drawer.

"Well, I'd better get the ham in the oven or it'll never be done in time. Are you sure I can't talk you into coming for dinner?" Sidney asked.

"I'll pass. I'm still not ready to be around Jackson." Nash took a step back. "I think I'll finish up the chores and go home, build a fire and watch movies all night."

"Sounds nice." What would it be like to snuggle on the couch with Nash in front of a roaring fire? Sidney tried to push the thought out of his mind. *It'll never happen,* he told himself.

"Not nice, but enough." Nash tucked the Christmas card in his coat pocket. "Thanks again for the present."

"I've already given the guy your address, so he'll ship them as soon as they're ready. Let me know if they don't fit or something's wrong with them."

Nash pulled on his gloves. "They'll be perfect, and I'll wear them with pride."

* * * *

After setting up a comfortable, make-shift spot to read, Nash drew the heavy sleeping bag over his lap. He glanced at Diablo through the slats in the stall door before picking up his book.

It was only the sixth evening sitting with the frightened horse, and already Nash could tell a difference in Diablo's temperament towards him. Nash didn't attempt to engage Diablo in any way other than to occasionally talk to himself out loud.

As he tried to concentrate on his book, Sidney kept coming to mind. Jackson had left earlier in the day to head back to Colorado. Nash couldn't quite figure out why it was so important for Jackson to return to a feed lot on New Year's Eve. Still, at least the man had spent the previous day with his son.

Nash shook his head. He still couldn't believe Sidney was twenty-one. He just hoped the man was smart about drinking. It wasn't that Nash didn't drink—he enjoyed alcohol in moderation—but he'd seen far too many people lose their good sense once alcohol entered the picture.

He reached for his thermos and realised he'd left it in the truck. "Shit." With a resigned sigh, Nash set down his book. He threw off the sleeping bag before getting to his feet. "Be right back," he told Diablo.

Nash opened the barn door and automatically glanced up at Sidney's window. He hadn't expected to see the younger man, but there he was, sitting on the window seat, cigarette in hand with that damn sweater wrapped around him.

Sidney wasn't looking down at Nash—instead he seemed to be staring at something in the room. Nash reigned in his desire to rush to Sidney's side. It wasn't until he watched Sidney wipe his eyes that he decided to act on his feelings.

He shut the barn door before heading to the house. It was a toss-up as to whether or not he'd be welcomed. He'd spoken very little to Sidney since Christmas. Most of Nash's days had been taken up with chores and Diablo, but it was more than that. He hadn't trusted himself to spend any more time with Sidney.

Stepping into the house, Nash shed his coat and boots. As he raced up the staircase, he tried to remember why he needed to stay away from Sidney. He'd already admitted to himself he was in love with the younger man, so whether they slept together or not it wouldn't make it any easier to say goodbye when the spring semester started.

He knocked once on Sidney's closed door before opening it. "You okay?"

Sidney shook his head while blowing his nose. "I hate him."

Nash crossed the room and sat beside Sidney on the window seat. He didn't need to ask who Sidney was talking about. "What happened?" he asked, taking off his hat.

"He told me not to come back this summer unless I got a

haircut and straightened up my act. And by that, he really meant I have to *straighten* up my sex life."

"You told him?"

Sidney nodded and reached for another tissue. "I shouldn't have, but he pissed me off so I just blurted it out. Now he hates me even more than he did before."

Nash couldn't take it. Sidney's tears shattered any reservations he had left. He pulled the smaller man into his arms. "Shhh." He wished he could tell Sidney it wasn't true, but how could he? In all the years he'd known the Wilks family, never once had he witnessed Jackson act even remotely loving towards his son.

At a loss for words, Nash remained silent. He kissed the top of Sidney's head and rubbed his back as the younger man continued to cry. Sidney had never been what Nash would consider a crybaby, so the tears proved to him how Jackson's words had hurt him.

Nash had witnessed Jackson's tirades towards his son on more than one occasion, and although Sidney refused to meet Jackson's gaze while being dressed down, never had he cried.

"I'm sorry," Sidney said, pulling back. He went to reach for another tissue, but Nash beat him to it.

Nash took hold of Sidney's chin and wiped his nose. "Don't apologise to me. You've suffered more than anyone I've ever known. If anyone deserves to break down, it's you." He pulled another tissue out of the box and tried to wipe away the black eyeliner that streaked Sidney's cheeks.

Sidney surprised Nash with a laugh, but seemed mortified when snot shot from his nose. "Oh my God, I can't believe I just did that." He dived for a fresh tissue before turning his back on Nash to blow his nose.

For some reason Nash found the entire event endearing. He leant over and kissed the side of Sidney's neck. "You're too cute for your own good."

By the time Sidney turned back around, he seemed to have his emotions under control. "You really think I'm cute?"

The expression on Sidney's face when he asked the question told Nash what words couldn't. "No, well, yeah, but I also happen to think you're sexy. Does that help?"

Sidney nodded. "How sexy?"

With a chuckle, Nash scooped Sidney into his arms. He stood and walked towards the bed. "So sexy that it's driving me crazy."

Sidney's green eyes were huge with surprise when Nash tossed him onto the bed. "What're you doing?"

Nash unbuttoned his shirt before joining Sidney in bed. "I don't know. Maybe you can help me figure it out."

"Now you decide to do this? Now, when I'm all puffy and snotty?"

Closing his eyes, Nash brushed his lips over Sidney's. The contact was electrifying. It didn't take a genius to figure out why. Nash had finally fallen completely in love with Sidney. He sighed when he felt the tip of Sidney's tongue tickle his bottom lip.

Nash opened his mouth as he buried his fingers in Sidney's hair. After several incredible moments, he took over the kiss. He couldn't seem to get enough as his tongue plundered Sidney's mouth, touching each tooth and ridge. His body was on fire. Nash struggled for several moments with his shirt before finally breaking the kiss. He rose up on his knees and untangled his hands from the cuffs of his shirt. "Need to feel you."

Sidney brushed his hands across his chest. "Good idea. I'm not sure Mom would approve of you fucking me in her sweater."

Nash popped the button on his jeans and grinned. "Your mom liked me."

Sidney took over and lowered the zipper on Nash's jeans. Before releasing Nash's cock, he ran his hand over the thick erection still trapped within the confines of Nash's underwear.

"Take it out," Nash said with a thrust of his hips. He realised his hands were shaking and hid them from view by pressing them to the small of his back.

Sidney carefully freed Nash's cock, pushing the underwear down below Nash's balls. "Please tell me I can suck this?"

With a nod, Nash directed the head of his cock towards Sidney's mouth. "Yeah. I don't plan on coming in your mouth anyway."

After several swipes of his tongue, Sidney took the crown in his mouth. Nash stared into Sidney's eyes as the man worked his way up and down on Nash's dick. It was obvious Sidney knew exactly what he was doing, a fact that disturbed Nash more than he wanted to admit. Who were the men he'd learnt his skills on? Did he still see them at school?

Nash shook his head. It was a big reminder of why he'd resisted for so long. Soon Sidney would be gone, and Nash would be left to worry. Sex was a natural part of college life. Isn't that what Reece had told him? So it would stand to reason Sidney would fall back into the sexual way of life once he returned to Pennsylvania.

Sidney encircled the base of Nash's cock before letting the length slip from his mouth. "What's wrong?"

"Nothing. Feels good," Nash replied, trying to hide his jealousy. It was fucking ridiculous that he could get upset over something that hadn't even happened yet.

"You want me to get some lube?" Sidney asked, rubbing Nash's balls.

Nash continued to stare down at Sidney. *What am I doing?* With a groan of frustration, Nash moved to sit on the edge of the bed with his back to Sidney. "I..."

"Oh no you don't. You're the one who started this. Don't fucking back out on me," Sidney said, pushing against Nash's back.

"What happens when you go back to school?" Nash felt the bed dip as Sidney moved. Several moments later, bare skin pressed against his back as Sidney's arms draped over Nash's shoulders.

"Then I'll miss you even more than I already do when I'm

away," Sidney whispered in Nash's ear.

"I've heard what it's like at college. And even though I know it's part of the experience, the thought of you having sex with other men..." Nash was unable to finish the thought.

Sidney crawled off the bed to stand in front of Nash. He quickly removed his sweatpants before straddling Nash's lap. "My roommate, Josh, makes fun of me constantly because I refuse to go out with anyone more than six times." Sidney brushed a kiss across Nash's mouth. "You know why?"

Nash shook his head. "Because you have so many men to choose from you're anxious to move on?" Just the thought made Nash's stomach hurt.

"Nope. I limit the dates because I know there's no point in misleading a guy into believing there's a chance for something more. You see, I've already found the man I want to spend my life with." Sidney kissed Nash again, deeper than before. "I've spent the last three years trying to figure out a way to get you to notice me as more than a little buddy. Now that I have, what more can I ask for?"

Although it wasn't a declaration of love, Nash felt better. He ran his hands down Sidney's slim, knobby back to tickle the top of his crack. Forever wasn't something Nash had even let himself hope for, but hearing the words gave him pause. Would it be fair of him to ask Sidney to commit to an exclusive long distance relationship? *No.*

With everything Sidney had been through in his life, the younger man deserved to experience all that the world had to offer. Besides, being in love still didn't make it possible for the two of them to reconcile their different goals in life.

Nash could easily see their future laid out before him. They would continue their on-again-off-again relationship until Sidney graduated from college, but then what? Sidney would get a job at some big fancy architectural firm in the city and Nash would visit when he wasn't busy with the ranch? What kind of life would that be for either of them?

"I can't do it," Nash mumbled. "I'm sorry, but we both know there's no future for us."

Sidney scrambled off Nash's lap. "I don't know anything of the sort. Who're you to decide what my future holds?"

Nash hated himself for hurting Sidney, but he was older. And if it took him being the asshole in order to make sure Sidney got everything in life he deserved, Nash would deal with it. How, he wasn't sure, but doing what was best for Sidney seemed more important than breaking his own heart.

Nash stood and tried to ignore Sidney as he retrieved his discarded jeans.

"You're leaving?"

Zipping up, Nash retrieved his hat from the window seat and settled it on his head. "I know it hurts now, but someday I hope you'll understand that I'm only pushing you away for your own good."

"What a crock of shit," Sidney spat, throwing Nash's shirt at him. "If you want to leave, leave, but don't you dare put it on me."

Shirt in hand, Nash moved to stand in front of Sidney. "I hope someday you'll forgive me."

"I doubt it," Sidney whispered before Nash walked out of the room.

71

Chapter Five

Sitting at his makeshift drafting table, which consisted of a sheet of plywood on top of his mattress, Sidney stared at the miniature totem pole on the shelf over his bed. It had been three weeks since he'd last seen Nash. Twenty-three days since he'd heard the low timbre of his cowboy's voice. Sidney sighed and dropped his head down on his clasped hands.

"Not again," Josh said, coming into the dorm room. "I thought you were over that asshole."

Sidney didn't bother looking up. "Leave me alone."

"Nope, not gonna happen." Josh bumped Sidney with his hip. "I'm dragging you to the cafeteria. You're starting to resemble a fucking skeleton. I walked in the room the other night and almost screamed like a girl when I caught you changing your clothes."

"That's just because you've never seen such a big cock before. It's okay. I won't hold your lack of experience against you." Although Sidney grumbled, he couldn't help but smile. Josh had a way of making him forget his problems, at least for a while.

Without warning, Josh unzipped his jeans and pulled his flaccid cock out. He waved the bigger than average penis in front of Sidney's face. It said a lot for Sidney's state of mind that the cock mere inches from his mouth didn't tempt him in the slightest. Of course it could have something to do with the fact his roommate was straight.

Sidney ignored Josh's cock and stared up into his eyes. "Are you kidding me? Are you really that comfortable in your heterosexuality that you'll tempt a gay man like that?"

Chuckling, Josh shoved his cock back into his underwear. Once he was zipped up, Josh leant down and ran a quick hand over the front of Sidney's jeans.

"What the fuck, man?" Sidney yelled, jumping to his feet.

"Just trying to gauge how depressed you are. I'll admit I may not have the biggest cock you've ever seen, but I'm damn sure it's the prettiest. If that did nothing for you, you're screwed. Maybe you should go talk to one of the counsellors or something?"

Sidney waved away Josh's concern. "I'll be fine once I stop missing him." God help him, Josh was forever trying to use his psychology crap on him. "And for future reference, I wouldn't go around flashing your cock to every patient you think might be depressed."

"Hey, I don't tell you how to draw buildings, so don't start telling me how to treat future patients," Josh said around a chuckle.

It took Sidney several minutes to find his sneakers in the piles of laundry that had gone unwashed since he'd returned to school, but he eventually found them. During the hunt, his jeans had started to slip down his lean hips. Sidney hiked them up before sitting down to put his shoes on. Josh was right. Sidney'd lost over eight pounds in the past three weeks. Eight pounds he couldn't afford to lose, but the thought of eating turned his stomach.

Evidently Josh noticed the action. "Hey, you want me to call home and see if my twelve-year-old brother has outgrown some of his clothes? I'm sure mom would be happy to send them to you."

"Ha ha." Sidney stood before pulling up his pants once again. It was getting ridiculous. He either needed to get over Nash and start eating again, or go shopping. Buying new clothes was infinitely easier. "Feel like going to the mall after dinner?"

"Hell, yeah."

Sidney's eyes narrowed as he stared at his friend. "Are you sure you're not gay?"

Josh grinned. "Luke's the one with the shopping gene. I got the scoping-for-pussy gene from my grandpa."

Just the word was enough to turn Sidney's stomach. How men could stick their...no, it was too gross to even think about. Although Josh rarely spoke of it, Sidney knew Josh's grandfather, the great Senator Edward Ballentine, had gone through six wives before dying at the age of sixty-eight of a heart attack. Josh had even confided that the Senator had died while in bed with an eighteen-year-old prostitute.

Sidney shook his coat to make sure the keys were still in the pocket. "Ready?"

"Right behind you," Josh answered.

* * * *

As the snow on the ranch slowly melted, Nash began to make headway with Diablo. The scarred and frightened horse still wouldn't let Nash ride him, but at least he no longer shied away from Nash's touch.

It had taken many days and nights of proving himself to the stallion, but as far as Nash was concerned, it would all be worth it in the end. Nash had no illusions of Diablo becoming the champion he was meant to be, but with time and patience perhaps the stallion would make money in stud fees.

He heard a truck pull into the yard and shut the corral gate before going to investigate. "Hey, Tommy," he greeted one of the seasonal ranch hands.

"Nash," Tommy returned with a tip of his hat. "Thought I'd come by and see if you need help now that the weather's warming up."

"Sure do," Nash answered. "I drew up a list of men to call just last night." He pulled the folded sheet of paper from his coat pocket. "Feel like startin' today?"

Tommy nodded. "I've been stuck inside so long I'm itching to get back to work."

Nash felt a little guilty for what he was about to do, but

he hated calling people. He held out the piece of paper. "You can start by calling everyone on this list. If they're not available, draw a line through their name, and we'll put an ad in the paper."

Tommy took the list and shoved it in his pocket. He seemed intent on digging a rut in the gravelled drive with the heel of his boot. It was obvious Tommy had something on his mind.

"Something else you wanted to say?" Nash asked.

Tommy took off his hat and finger-combed his hair out of his face before resetting it. "There's been talk in town about Sidney."

"What about him?"

"Word is, he's one of those funny fellas. Not that it matters, I'd just like to know in case there's a problem down the road," Tommy explained.

"What kind of problems do you expect, Tommy?" Nash asked. Outing Sidney wasn't something Nash was comfortable doing. If Sidney came back for summer break and wanted to address the ranch hands' concerns regarding his sexuality, Nash would support him all the way, but it wasn't Nash's place to do it for him.

Tommy shrugged. "You know folks around here. They're so bored with life they'll jump on anything or anyone that's different."

"Sidney's always been different, you know that. It's never bothered you before."

"And it doesn't bother me now. I just thought it'd be nice to know the truth. I meant no disrespect."

Nash's initial response was to jump down Tommy's throat, but he stopped himself. Tommy was a good guy. He'd worked for the Running E for four season, and Nash hoped to have his experience for many more. "We both know I'm not going to confirm or deny anything, right?"

Tommy blew out a breath. "Yeah. I get ya."

"Good." Nash gestured towards the barn. "You can use the phone in the tack room."

* * * *

"You're sure your mom doesn't mind me coming home with you?" Sidney asked.

"Shut up," Josh reached over and punched Sidney on the arm.

"Ow! Driving here," Sidney reminded his roommate. Normally Sidney would be headed back to Kansas for Spring Break, but not only had he refused to cut his hair, but he still hadn't spoken to Nash since he'd left after Winter Break.

"Come on, it'll be fun." Josh put his feet up on the dashboard of Sidney's four-year-old Malibu. "Besides, Luke'll be there."

"Would you stop that?"

"What?"

"Stop trying to fix me up with your brother. It isn't going to happen," Sidney said. Luke was hot, funny and athletic but he wasn't Nash. Sidney bit his bottom lip. No matter how many times he tried to get over his cowboy he couldn't do it. He'd spent the last couple of months living like a monk. Not because the offers hadn't been there, Sidney just hadn't been interested.

"I brought my camera this time so you'll have to go to downtown Philadelphia with me at some point so I can take pictures."

"You're the only person I know who'd rather take pictures of high rises. Philly's known for the old shit, man, not the new stuff."

"Yeah, well maybe I want pictures of both," Sidney countered. His dream was to design new high rises that had the charm and detail of the older buildings found in cities all over the country. Glass and chrome buildings were cool, but he doubted they'd stand the test of time. In fifty years the modern crap they were putting up would come down to make way for even more modern crap, but the old-style architecture would always be around.

"This one?" Sidney asked, gesturing to the exit.

"Yeah." Josh gave Sidney directions to the small upper-class West Chester neighbourhood just outside Philadelphia he'd grown up in.

Sidney pulled into the large circular drive. "This okay?"

"For now." Josh opened his door and slapped Sidney playfully on the back of the head. "Come on. I bet Mom's got something warm from the oven to fatten you up."

Sidney groaned. "Are you going to make fun of me all week or what?"

Josh slammed the door. He bounced from foot to foot like he was about to take Sidney on in a boxing match. Sidney shut his door and pocketed his keys. "How old are you?"

"Can't help it," Josh said with a laugh. "Something about being home brings out the kid in me."

Yes. Sidney had witnessed the byplay of the Ballentine brothers on several occasions. It usually started with Josh and worked its way around the house until all five Ballentine brothers were affected. "God help me."

"Mua ha ha ha. There's no help for you now, Sidney. You are about to step into the Ballentine lair," Josh said in a creepy voice Sidney wished he could forget.

The front door opened and Josh's mother came out to stand on the large brick landing. "Joshua!"

Josh gave his mom a hug and a kiss on the cheek. "Hey, Mom."

Mrs Ballentine released Josh and held her arms out to Sidney. "It's so good to see you."

Sidney paused. He'd never felt comfortable hugging people. *Nash was an exception.* Sidney silently cursed himself for once again going back to Nash. Not everything in his life had to revolve around the handsome cowboy. He climbed the brick steps and allowed Mrs Ballentine to hug him. After all, trying to get out of the customary greeting was a futile gesture. He'd learnt that the first time he'd joined the Ballentine's for Thanksgiving.

Mrs Ballentine, or Maggie as she insisted Sidney call her,

seemed to hold him over the required time for a polite greeting.

"Josh told me you've had a hard time lately. I hope you'll use this week to find your happy place once again," Maggie whispered in Sidney's ear.

Sidney narrowed his eyes at Josh, promising retribution. "I'm okay," he told her.

"Of course you are." Maggie released Sidney and held him at arm's length. "You look good."

"Don't lie to him, mom, he's skinny," Josh cut in.

Maggie patted Sidney's stomach. "Nothing a weeks' worth of home cooked meals can't fix."

If Maggie only knew the only home cooked meals he was used to getting were the ones he'd made himself, she'd probably never let him leave. Sidney smiled and nodded, keeping his mouth shut.

The first time he'd joined the Ballentines for Thanksgiving, Sidney had marvelled at the family dynamic. He couldn't imagine growing up in a house where sports and homework were the biggest topics around the dinner table. Rarely did Sidney's dad sit with him at the table and when he did there was never any conversation between the two of them.

Sidney had thought Josh had the perfect life until about the third day. After Josh's youngest brother, Eric, had burst into the bedroom for the thousandth time without knocking, Sidney began to think being an only child wasn't so bad.

"Give me the keys," Josh said, breaking into Sidney's thoughts.

"What?"

"Keys? You know, to get our suitcases?" Josh pantomimed opening the trunk.

Sidney pulled the keys out of his pocket before tossing them to Josh. "Will you grab mine, too?"

"Hear that Mom? He treats me like a slave!"

Maggie rolled her eyes. "Don't be so dramatic."

"Yeah, what she said." Sidney leant over and said in a stage whisper, "Are you really sure he's yours?"

"Sadly, yes. He gets his oddball sense of humour from his father." Maggie grinned. "No wonder I love him so much."

And thus his Spring Break had begun.

* * * *

Sidney swung back and forth on the double-wide hammock and watched Luke and Josh throw a football back and forth between them.

"I think we should go to Manhattan tomorrow," Josh said.

"Why?" Sidney asked, tucking the blanket around his feet. Evidently someone had forgotten to inform Philadelphia it was spring.

"Because I'm bored, and it'll give you a chance to take a billion pictures. Why don't you come with us, Luke?"

"No way I'm driving," Sidney added before Luke could answer.

"We usually take the train," Luke informed Sidney. "Yeah, I'll go along, but I bet Mom'll make us take Zac."

"No way. What if we want a beer or something? Zac's only nineteen."

"Are you planning to go bar hopping?" Sidney asked. "Because if that's the case, I'm out." Josh and Sidney's ideas of fun places to party were completely different.

"No, but if we decide to stop in somewhere and listen to some music..." Josh let the statement hang in the cold West Chester air.

"What kind of music?" Sidney knew he wasn't getting the full story.

"Okay, fine. You know that girl from my Sociology class that I told you about?"

"Veronica?" Sidney had listened to Josh talk non-stop about the buxom redhead since the beginning of the term.

"Yeah. Anyway, turns out she's in a band and they're playing at a place called Smokey Joe's on Friday night. Anyway, I thought if we went up for the day, we could stop in and listen for a few minutes," Josh explained.

Sidney glanced at Luke. Josh's older brother was staring straight at him. Evidently it was Sidney's decision whether to go or not. As much as he hated the thought of hanging out at a straight club all evening, Sidney couldn't bring himself to say no. "Fine."

"Cool." Josh tossed the football to Luke. "I'll go tell Mom and Dad."

As soon as Josh left, Luke chuckled. "I take it Veronica's not his usual."

Sidney nodded. "She hasn't given him the time of day and it's driving him nuts."

"It's good for him. Life's always been a breeze for Josh."

"And you?" Sidney asked. "What's life been like for you? I thought you were Mr Big Man on Campus?"

Luke sat in one of the chairs close to the hammock. "Yeah, well, sports have never been a problem for me. It's everything else."

Sidney could tell by the expression on Luke's face he wanted to talk, but didn't know where to begin. "Like how to tell your family you're gay?"

For a split second, Luke seemed surprised by the question, but he eventually nodded. "Yeah. And not just my family. I have coaches to answer to, teammates…hell, the list goes on and on."

Sidney reached out and laid a hand on Luke's knee. "I wouldn't worry about your family."

"Yours was cool?" Luke asked, hope in his eyes.

"Uhh, no, but my dad is nothing like yours. But I still don't regret telling him. I think, for me, it was a test more than anything."

"A test for what?"

"To see how much he loved me, or whether he even loved me at all," Sidney said, removing his hand. He snuggled under the blanket.

"And did he pass?" Luke asked.

Thinking back to the morning of the big fight with his dad, Sidney shook his head. "I'm still not sure. He told me not to bother coming home again unless I cut my hair and stopped wearing eyeliner."

"But it looks hot on you." Luke shut himself off and squirmed in his chair. "I mean, it's who you are."

Sidney warmed at the compliment. It had been a long time since he'd felt truly desirable. Sure he'd been asked out plenty of times since Winter Break, but he knew all that was required of him was a lubed ass. Not one of the guys who pursued him cared about anything but getting laid. "Yeah, well, I'm from a small town, so my dad wants me to blend in with the locals, I guess."

"Blend in? What a depressing thought."

Sidney smiled. "I agree, which is why I'm here in West Chester instead of back on the ranch."

Luke leant forward to rest his forearms on his knees. The new position showcased the broad expanse of his chest. Sidney nearly swooned. Luke was almost as big as Nash. "Stop it," he mumbled under his breath.

"Excuse me?"

"Nothing." Once again, Sidney tried to push all thoughts of Nash to the background.

Luke stared at Sidney for several moments before standing. "I'm gonna go grab some lunch. Hungry?"

"Sure." Sidney wasn't, but maybe it would help to get his mind off Nash and back onto the handsome man in front of him.

* * * *

With a big, goofy, drunken grin on his face, Josh waved the napkin with Veronica's phone number on it in front of Sidney's face. "I told you it would be worth all the hassle."

Sidney knocked Josh's hand away before pulling to the side of the road. He looked into the rear view mirror at Luke. "Do me a favour and change places with this drunken idiot before I kill him."

Josh might be happy, but Sidney was anything but. Not

only had they ended up driving his car to Newark before catching a cab into New York City, but the band Veronica was in was some kind of punk grunge crap. Sidney had a splitting headache, and a drunk waving shit in his face was the last straw.

"Aw, Sid, don't you love me anymore?" Josh said, leaning over the console to kiss Sidney's cheek.

"I'll love you tomorrow. Tonight I hate your guts. Now get your ass in the backseat." Sidney pushed Josh towards the door Luke held open.

Josh started laughing and dived into the back seat through the split in the front bucket seats. Sidney rolled his eyes at Luke once he was buckled in in the front passenger seat.

"Cut him some slack," Luke said with a grin. "He's a happy boy. Haven't you ever been around Josh when he was drunk?"

"Yeah, but I'm usually drunk, too." Sidney checked for traffic before pulling back onto the highway.

"I told you I'd drive if you wanted to drink," Luke reminded Sidney.

Sidney glanced in the rear view mirror. Josh seemed to be out like a light. He turned his attention back to Luke. "I know you did, but I didn't wanna drink around you." Sidney's afternoon with Luke had been everything he'd hoped for. Luke was funny and shy, and so fucking adorable that Sidney hadn't thought of Nash once all day. Well, except for just then but that didn't count.

Taking a huge chance, Sidney reached over and covered Luke's hand. "Thanks. I had a great time with you."

Luke turned his hand over and threaded his fingers through Sidney's. He twisted around to look in the back seat. "He's passed out."

Sidney smiled. "I know."

Luke cleared his throat. "I was wondering…um…would you go out with me some time?"

It was a huge step for Luke to take, and Sidney knew it. Suddenly, Sidney wanted to feel Luke's lips on his. He couldn't explain it, but he knew if he kissed Luke just once he'd know whether or not things could work between them.

"Have you ever kissed a guy?" Sidney asked.

Luke chuckled. "I've never kissed anyone who wasn't family."

Sidney gave Luke's hand a gentle tug. "Crawl over here and let me be the first."

Luke checked the back seat once more before unbuckling his seat belt. "You're not going to, like, grade me or anything, are you?"

Sidney laughed. "No, nothing like that." He gripped the steering wheel with his left hand. There was very little traffic and they were cruising down a fairly straight highway, so he felt comfortable burying the fingers of his right hand in Luke's short, thick hair as he brought their lips together.

Sidney groaned. The urge to close his eyes and sink into the kiss was overwhelming, but his present situation couldn't accommodate his body's desires. A flash of brown ahead on the road got his attention. He broke the kiss and tried to push Luke back into his seat, but it was too late. Sidney hit the deer going at sixty-five miles an hour.

The last thing he remembered was a searing pain in his chest plus the sound of glass shattering.

Chapter Six

Nash sat at Sidney's bedside and continued to curse Jackson. Although Nash was grateful he'd been called after the car accident, he couldn't help but wonder where Jackson was.

Nash had been sound asleep when he'd received the phone call from Jackson. His boss explained that Sidney had been in a serious car wreck and had been taken to a hospital in Trenton, New Jersey, and he needed Nash to fly to New Jersey until he could get there.

When Nash questioned Jackson as to why he couldn't just hop on a plane, Jackson had told him he was vacationing in Hawaii and wouldn't be able to get a flight out right away. The whole thing stank as far as Nash was concerned. Jackson had the money to hire a private plane if he wanted, so why the fuck wasn't he?

Sidney groaned, causing Nash to jump to his feet and lean over the hospital bed. "Sidney?"

Instead of opening his eyes, Sidney fell back into the deep sleep he'd been in since Nash had arrived four hours earlier. Staring down at the younger man, Nash was hard pressed to recognise him.

From what he understood, the deer Sidney had struck with his car had come through the windshield. The impact had done severe damage to the car and two of its occupants. The young man in the passenger side seat, Luke Ballentine, had suffered a traumatic head injury when he was thrown from the car. The passenger in the back seat, Sidney's roommate, Josh, was unharmed except for a few minor cuts and scratches.

Nash was grateful Sidney had actually worn a seatbelt for a change, saving him from grave injuries, but it hadn't saved him completely. The bandages wrapped around Sidney's head kept Nash from seeing the full extent of the cuts, but the swollen and bruised face of the sleeping man looked nothing like the Sidney he loved. A row of stitches stretched from the corner of Sidney's mouth across his cheek to his earlobe.

Nash knew from speaking with the doctor that Sidney's body below the sheet was just as damaged. Thankfully, other than the mass of scars that would need time to heal, the doctor didn't believe there would be any permanent physical damage.

Nash turned and picked up his empty coffee cup. As much as he wanted to see those beautiful green eyes he'd fallen in love with, he knew the longer Sidney slept, the better. He left the room in search of coffee and answers.

He stepped up to the nurses' station. "Excuse me?"

A nurse looked up. "May I help you, sir?"

"Yes, Ma'am. I was wondering if you can tell me anything about the condition of the other two men who were brought in with Sidney Wilks?"

The nurse bit her bottom lip. "I'm not allowed, but the family's in the waiting room, just through those doors."

Nash smiled. "Thanks." He hit the button and waited for the automatic doors to open. Nash stood in the entrance to the small waiting room. What should he say to the gathered group? The red puffy eyes of everyone in the family told Nash something was wrong.

The only woman in the room glanced up and met his gaze. She stood without saying a word before approaching. "Are you Sidney's family?"

Nash swallowed around the lump in his throat. "I'm Nash. I work for Sidney's father."

The attractive woman reached out and touched Nash's arm. "I'm Maggie, Josh and Luke's mother." Tears filled Maggie's eyes. "I'm sorry we haven't been down to check on Sidney. How is he?"

Two of the young men joined them, standing like guards on either side of their mother. Nash wondered if one of them was Josh.

"He'll have scars, but he'll heal. How're your boys?"

Maggie pointed across the room to a man who had his back to Nash. "Josh will be just fine. He has a bump on his head and a few scrapes. Nothing serious though, thank God."

Nash started to ask about Luke but kept his mouth shut and waited for Maggie to go on. Although he knew they had their own to worry about, Nash couldn't help but wonder why Josh hadn't at least checked on Sidney.

"Luke..." she began, but a sudden burst of emotion stopped her from going further.

One of the young men put his arm around his mom. "Luke just got out of surgery. The doctors aren't optimistic, but we are. Aren't we, Mom?"

Maggie nodded and squeezed her son's hand. "Yes. It takes more than a skull fracture and broken back to keep a Ballentine down."

Nash could tell by the emotion on Maggie's face she didn't believe her own statement. It was obvious the family was trying to be strong. "Is there anything I can do for you? I could find a deli or something and bring you all back something to eat?" he offered.

Maggie shook her head. "Thank you, dear, but I doubt any of us has the stomach for food at the moment."

Nash hated feeling so distant with people Sidney cared so much for. A handsome middle-aged man came into the room, his blue eyes rimmed in red. "Would you like to go in and sit with him?" he asked Maggie.

Maggie nodded before wiping her nose with a tissue. "Please let us know when Sidney is strong enough for visitors," she told Nash.

"I will," he promised.

"Alan, this is Nash, Sidney's friend," Maggie introduced

him.

Alan held out his hand and Nash shook it. "How's Sidney?"

"He has a long way to go, but he'll heal." Nash almost felt guilty giving the Ballentine family the optimistic prognosis. He wondered how bad Luke really was. His gaze went back to Josh, who had still refused to even turn and look at Nash. *Does he know how much I hurt Sidney?* Perhaps Josh hated him.

Nash held up his empty cup. "I'd better fill up and get back to the room. Please, let me know if there's anything I can do." He glanced at Josh once more before leaving the room. As he strode towards the vending machine, Nash's hands began to shake. What if it had been Sidney who had gone through the windshield instead of Luke?

* * * *

After spending the night in a reclining chair in the corner of the room, Nash woke to voices. He sprang up before his eyes were fully opened. "Sidney?" He received a grunt in reply.

Nash focussed on the man standing beside Sidney's bed. "When did you get in?"

"A few minutes ago," Jackson answered.

Two days. It had taken Jackson over sixty hours after receiving the call to get his ass to the hospital. Nash ran his fingers through his hair before going to stand on the other side of Sidney's bed. "You need a drink?"

Sidney blinked twice.

Nash picked up the plastic water pitcher and held it out to Jackson. "Take this to the little room down the hall and fill it up with ice and water."

"Can't he talk?" Jackson asked, taking the pitcher.

"He can, but it hurts when the stitches pull." Nash reached down and brushed the back of Sidney's hand. "It'll just take a few more days, right?" he asked Sidney.

Sidney blinked twice.

Nash gestured towards the pitcher. "If you need help ask one of the nurses." As soon as Jackson left the room, Nash bent over. "You okay?"

Sidney blinked once, tears pooling in his eyes.

"Shhh, no crying. You know how much those damn things sting." Nash grabbed a tissue off the table and dabbed at Sidney's eyes.

Sidney pointed at the small pad of paper. Other than yes or no answers, writing had become Sidney's way of communicating.

Nash moved the bed tray over Sidney before handing him the pen.

Luke? Sidney wrote.

Nash shook his head. "He's still in a coma." He didn't want to tell Sidney that the doctors doubted Luke would ever wake up from his deep sleep.

Josh?

"I saw him last night. Maggie was trying to get the boys to go home and get a good night's sleep." Nash had promised himself he would confront Josh about not coming in to check on Sidney. He'd tried to be patient. Tried to understand Josh had his brother to worry about, but what about Sidney?

"It's nice that your dad's here though. Maybe I should leave the two of you alone for a while."

Sidney's pen went to work on the paper. *No! I need you here.*

Even on paper, the statement warmed Nash. "How about this? I'll go find a cheap hotel and check in long enough to shower and change. I'll be back in a few hours. Okay?"

Again, Sidney scribbled on the pad. *I don't know what to say to him.*

"Then don't say anything." Nash grinned and touched Sidney's chin. "You've got the perfect excuse."

Check on Josh and Luke?

"I will." Nash leant down and pressed a soft kiss to

Sidney's cheek. "I won't be gone long."

Jackson came back into the room. "Here." He held the pitcher out to Nash.

Although Nash would be more than happy to take care of Sidney, he felt it was time Jackson took some responsibility. "Fill up his cup and hold the straw to his mouth. When he's had enough, he'll hold up his hand."

Nash grabbed the pad of paper before ripping off the used sheet. It wasn't any of Jackson's business what he and Sidney had talked about. He shoved the paper in his pocket before setting the pad back down in front of Sidney. "Get some rest if you can."

Sidney blinked twice as he opened his mouth for the straw.

Leaving the room, Nash spotted Maggie in the hall. "Any change?"

Maggie shook her head. "The swelling's gone down in his brain, but he still hasn't come out of the coma. How's Sidney?"

"He's doing okay. His dad just got here." Nash stuck his hands in his coat pockets. "Can I ask you something?"

"Sure," Maggie answered.

"Sidney keeps asking about Josh. Do you think you could get him to stop by and say hi to Sidney today?"

Maggie looked to the side. "Josh's barely said a word since the accident." She shook her head. "Although physically he came out almost unscathed, I don't think I can say the same for his emotional well-being." Maggie reached out and laid a hand on Nash's arm. "I'll stop in and check on Sidney and tell him what I just told you. Hopefully Sidney will understand."

Nash nodded. What else could he say?

* * * *

Sidney opened his eyes from a nap to find the room empty. He glanced at the clock on the wall. He'd only been asleep for forty minutes, so where had his dad gone? *Just as well*, he told himself. It was still hard for him to realise his dad knew so little about him.

One of Jackson's first questions had been who the two men were who had been in the accident with Sidney. When Sidney had written Josh and Luke's names on a sheet of paper, his dad didn't act like he knew them. Sidney went back and wrote *roommate* next to Josh's name.

"Oh," his dad had said. "That's the kid you spend holidays with sometimes."

Sidney had blinked twice, but his dad wasn't looking at him, so he'd had to write the word 'yes' on the paper.

Looking towards the door, Sidney wondered why Josh hadn't been in. According to Nash, Josh had made it through the wreck with minor injuries. He understood that Luke's condition was far more serious than his own, but surely Josh had time to stop in for a minute at least.

Sidney's chest tightened. What if Josh knew? What if he'd been coherent enough to witness the kiss? Sidney silently cursed himself. It was his fault Luke hadn't been belted in. He knew he'd live with that guilt for the rest of his life. It drove him crazy that he couldn't get out of bed and check on Luke and Josh for himself, but he was trapped in this fucking room.

Pushing the button on the bed rail, Sidney slowly raised himself to a sitting position. The stitches in his back screamed in protest, but he had a letter to write. He picked up the pen and stared at the blank sheet of paper.

Josh,
I miss you. Please come in to see me. I'm sorry about the accident. Sorry I let you down. Most of all, I'm sorry Luke's hurt. Please forgive me.
-Sidney

After setting his pen down, Sidney tore off the sheet of paper. He folded the note and wrote Josh's name on the outside before pushing the call button. He scribbled a quick note to the nurse while he waited.

Several moments later, the nurse came in. "Yes?"

He gave the woman both pieces of paper. She read his note and nodded. "I'll see what I can do."

Sidney laid back. He'd done all he could for the moment. What would he do if Josh never forgave him? He could feel himself sinking into a funk, and why shouldn't he? He hadn't been given a mirror to look at himself, but it was obvious from the pain he felt, even with the help of some really good drugs, that his face and body were a mess. *I'll look on the outside like I feel on the inside.*

"Miss me?" Nash asked, coming into the room.

Sidney stared up at the hopeful face of the man he loved. His vision clouded with emotion as he tried to imagine what Nash saw when he looked down at him. Did he see the battered shell of the man he used to find attractive, or did Nash see deeper, to the dark soul of the man who'd nearly killed himself and two others for a kiss that meant nothing?

"Do you know where Jackson went?" Nash asked.

Sidney blinked once.

Nash sighed and sat in the chair beside Sidney. "I spoke to your doctor. He said as long as you keep that ointment on your stitches you should be okay to talk. He encouraged it, actually."

Sidney blinked once. There was nothing he wanted to say. If he started talking, Nash would end up asking him how the accident had happened, and Sidney wasn't quite ready to admit it was his fault to anyone but himself.

Nash squeezed Sidney's hand. "I'm gonna go find Jackson. The doctor said you should be out of here in a few days, and there are plans that need to be made."

Sidney hadn't thought of what he'd do once released. The idea of his dad staying at home to take care of him was preposterous. He grabbed the pen and scribbled on the pad. *I can take care of myself.*

Instead of yelling at him, Nash stood and leaned close to Sidney's face. "I've no doubt you can, but you shouldn't have to, not when you have someone who loves you nearby."

Sidney wrote another note. *Dad won't stay.*

Nash glanced at the paper and shook his head. "I wasn't talking about Jackson."

Tears once again threatened. Sidney began to wonder if his emotional state had something to do with the pain medication he was being given. There had to be a reason other than the obvious. He blinked his eyes, quickly dispelling the moisture.

What the fuck was wrong with him? Nash had just professed his love. A sudden thought hit him. Was it brotherly love or the kind of love he really wanted? And would Nash still feel the same if he knew he'd lured a man out of his seatbelt minutes before hitting a deer? Then there were the scars. Sidney reached up and ran a finger across his cheek. He came away with the gooey antibiotic ointment covering his finger.

Nash grabbed Sidney's hand. "You're not supposed to touch it." He reached back to get a tissue from the table. After cleaning Sidney's finger, Nash kissed it. "I've done a lot of thinking in the last few days."

Sidney swallowed around the lump in his throat as Nash squeezed his hand.

"My purpose in life is to love you. When I thought I might lose you…"

Sidney sucked in a breath as he watched a tear roll down Nash's handsome face. Never had he seen Nash actually cry. "I'm still here," Sidney whispered.

The words seemed to make things worse. Nash dropped his chin to rest against his chest as he cried. Sidney lifted his hand and brushed Nash's hair away from his face. It was his turn to comfort the man who had always been there for him.

Nash eventually dried his eyes on his sleeve and looked

at Sidney. "I want another chance. I'll do whatever it takes."

Before Sidney could say or write what was in his heart, his dad strode into the room. Jackson took one look at Nash and stopped dead in his tracks. "What's wrong?"

Nash stood and shook his head. "Nothing. I was just telling Sidney how thankful I am that he'll be okay."

Jackson's gaze went from Nash to Sidney. "Of course we're thankful." He shifted from foot to foot. "Can I talk to you for a minute?" he asked Nash.

"Sure." Nash smiled down at Sidney. "Be right back."

Sidney watched Nash leave. Although he understood why Nash hadn't told Jackson the truth about their conversation, it still bothered him. Would Nash forever be in the closet? What kind of life could Sidney hope to have with the gorgeous cowboy if Nash continued to worry what others thought of their relationship? Hell, Sidney wasn't even sure what to call what he and Nash were starting. Relationship sounded long term. Was it possible the two of them could find a way to be together forever?

Sidney stared at the overhead light. Maybe Nash had been right. Perhaps their lives were too different to make it work.

The door opened and Josh stepped into the room. He stood staring at Sidney for several moments without saying a word. It was Sidney who finally broke the silence. "How's Luke?"

Josh shook his head. "He might as well be dead." He took several steps towards the bed as he continued to stare.

By the expression on Josh's face, Sidney wondered just how bad he really looked. Nash had assured him he would heal, but suddenly Sidney wanted to pull the sheet over his head to avoid Josh's gaze.

Josh held up the note Sidney had written. "I don't want or need your apologies. I just came in to tell you I can't talk to you for a while. I have some things I need to work out before I can do that. I've got your number."

Without another word, Josh turned and left the room.

Sidney stared at the door in a state of shock. Had he just lost his best friend?

* * * *

Nash followed Jackson to the hospital cafeteria.

"Coffee?" Jackson asked.

"Sure, I guess." Nash found a table while Jackson went to the serving line. What would Jackson say if he knew Nash had just told Sidney he loved him? Had his emotions been obvious? Maybe that's why Jackson wanted to speak with him alone.

Jackson set Nash's coffee in front of him before taking a seat at the small table. "We need to talk about what happens when we get Sidney home," he began.

"Yeah, I meant to talk to you about that."

Jackson sighed heavily and ran his hand over the back of his neck. "There's something you should know."

"Okay." Nash's whole body tensed.

"I was in Hawaii with my wife," Jackson said, leaning his crossed arms on the table.

"You're married?" It was the last thing Nash expected to hear.

"Yeah."

Nash finally understood why Jackson spent the majority of his time in Colorado, but where did that leave Sidney? "You're not planning to take Sidney back to Colorado, are you?"

Jackson readjusted his tall, lanky frame in the chair. "Sheila doesn't know about Sidney."

"Excuse me? How could you not've told her you have a son?"

"She's a very religious woman. I'm afraid she wouldn't understand him, and Sidney would just wind up getting hurt."

Nash flattened his palms on the table and leant forward. "So how could you possibly marry a woman who wouldn't

94

approve of your own son?"

"Because I love her," Jackson replied, his voice cool.

More than he loved Sidney, obviously. Something suddenly dawned on Nash. "Wait a minute. You said Sheila's worked for you for five years?"

"Yeah."

"You led me to believe you'd only owned the feedlot for a couple of years. Not only that, but how the hell could the woman work for you for that long and not know you had a son? What, were you ashamed of Sidney when he was only sixteen?"

Jackson shook his head. "First of all, I didn't tell you about the feedlot because it's none of your business. And secondly, Sheila's a decent, God-fearing woman. You and I've known since he was a boy that Sidney wasn't right in the head."

"Wasn't right? So you're telling me you think being queer is a mental condition?"

Jackson shrugged, giving Nash an answer without words.

Nash began to shake with unleashed fury. "I'm queer, too. You think I'm crazy?"

Jackson's eyes narrowed. "That the reason you've been sniffing around Sidney all these years?"

Nash couldn't control himself any longer. He reached across the table and grabbed the front of Jackson's shirt. "Listen here, you son-of-a-bitch , what I did for Sidney was give him a role model. Someone he could depend on, since you were never around. So don't you dare sit there and accuse me of impropriety when it sounds like I'm the only person alive who loves him."

Jackson glanced down at the front of his shirt. "If I could have fired your ass, I would've done so ten years ago, now I suggest you let me loose before I come over the table and show you how a real man fights."

Nash had at least forty pounds of solid muscle on Jackson, so the threat meant absolutely nothing. Still... "What did you mean by that? Why can't you fire me?"

Jackson's lips thinned and turned white. It was obvious the man hadn't meant to say what he did.

"You'd better start talking," Nash growled, releasing Jackson's shirt.

"Because despite all the hard work I've put into the fucking place, I'm only a trustee of the Running E. I earn a good salary as set forth in Elizabeth's will, but I don't own it. I don't know what kind of spell you cast over my wife when she was sick, but she made a provision that you were to be given use of her father's house and a job for as long as you wanted it."

"Maybe your wife realised what a lousy father you are and wanted someone around Sidney who was capable of love and compassion," he fired back. There were so many things wrong with Jackson's explanation, Nash wasn't sure where to begin. "So, Sidney owns the Running E?"

"Yes, but we both know he doesn't care about the ranch."

"He's twenty-one. Don't you think he has a legal right to know the truth?"

"Sure, but are you really ready to lose your job? Because we both know how much he hates Bridgewater. He'll sell as soon as he finds out the truth."

Nash shook his head. "Regardless, it's not your decision to make." With his mind made up, Nash stood. "I'll tell you what. I'll get Sidney back to the ranch so he can heal. Why don't you clear out of the house and move on up to Colorado to be with your new wife. We don't need you."

"Who the hell do you think you are? You can't order me out of my house," Jackson argued.

Nash noticed they were beginning to draw stares from the others in the area. "Maybe not, but Sidney can. Should I go up and tell him all your dirty little secrets?" It was the last thing Nash wanted to do. Sure, Sidney deserved the truth about the ranch, but not about his father's deceit. Knowing how ashamed Jackson was of his son would hurt Sidney more than Jackson was worth.

"Fine, but let me handle this my way, and keep your

grubby hands off my son until I clear out."

"You have four days. Sidney should be released in two, that'll give you two more to gather your shit."

grubby hand off my son until I clear out.

"You have four days, Si, they should be released in two, that'll give you two more to gather your stuff."

Chapter Seven

Sidney was surprised when Nash pulled up outside his house instead of the ranch house. "Aren't you taking me home?" He'd had the stitches in his face removed before leaving the hospital, but he still had to wait a few more days for the ones on his head and body to come out.

"Maybe later in the week once I know Jackson's gone. For now you'll have to settle for my humble abode." Nash got out of the truck.

Sidney waited until his door was opened before reaching to unfasten his seatbelt. It took him a moment to realise he wasn't wearing one. They'd tried buckling him in before leaving the airport in Wichita, but the old seatbelt rode too tight across Sidney's chest for comfort. Nash had ended up driving home on the back roads so he could go as slowly as he needed.

Nash had told Sidney Jackson was moving to Colorado permanently right after he'd broken the news that Sidney owned the Running E. It was still a shock to Sidney, even two days later. Sidney couldn't help but wonder why his mom had done it. Unbeknownst to Nash, Sidney planned to find a way to change the will once again.

Despite being barely twenty-one, Sidney's close brush with death had him thinking. If something had happened to him, it was important that the ranch be left in the hands of Nash, not Jackson. He promised himself to remedy the situation as soon as he was physically able to go into town.

Nash helped Sidney out of the truck. Spring in Kansas meant one thing, mud, and Sidney wasted no time stepping into a deep puddle of it. He lifted his foot and lost his sneaker in the process. "Great."

Nash picked Sidney up in his arms, taking care not to hurt Sidney any more than necessary. "What about my shoe?" Sidney asked, wincing as Nash's hold stretched his stitches.

"I'll unbury it in a few minutes." Nash carried Sidney to the small front porch before setting him on his feet. He unlocked and opened the door. "Home sweet home."

Sidney hadn't been inside the house since his grandfather was alive. He had to have only been around six or seven. "It looks so much smaller than I remember."

With his hands on his hips, Nash seemed to study the living room. "Can't imagine why a single guy would need more room."

Sidney gestured towards the corner of the living room. "Mom slept on a twin bed in that corner growing up."

"One person living here is one thing, but I can't imagine three."

"Wasn't three for long. My grandma died not long after Mom was born." Sidney shrugged. "Guess women in my family get the shaft when it comes to growing old."

Nash reached out and placed a gentle hand on Sidney's back. "It sounds like it. I'm sorry."

Now that they were finally back in Kansas, Sidney wanted what he'd been waiting for all week. "Can I use your shower?"

With a broad smile, Nash nodded. "I was going to suggest it, but I was afraid you'd take it the wrong way."

Sidney took off the loose baseball cap he'd put on before leaving the hospital and shook his head. With a silent curse, he realised he no longer had enough hair to shake. He'd been shaved to a barely-there stubble even shorter than his dad used to cut it. He noticed Nash's worrisome expression and quickly tried to cover. "You don't have to tell me I'm gross. I can smell myself."

"Hang on a second, and I'll bring in that soap the doctor suggested."

Sidney turned and kissed Nash on the chin. "Thank you

for bringing me here."

Nash wrapped his arms loosely around Sidney and kissed him. Sidney had hoped for one of Nash's deep kisses, but they both knew Sidney's healing face wasn't up to a wide-mouthed tongue battle yet.

"Go on in to the bathroom and get undressed. I'll bring your stuff in."

Sidney did as Nash suggested, stripping out of his clothes. He pulled the shower curtain back far enough to turn on the spray before turning to catch his reflection in the mirror. Just like the one in the hospital, the bathroom mirror only afforded Sidney a look at himself from the chest up. He tilted his head from side to side, studying several crisscrossing scars on the sides and top of his head.

"I'm a freak," he whispered. "Edward Scissorhands has nothing on me."

Sidney turned around and stepped up onto the edge of the bathtub. He grabbed the shower curtain rod with one hand and braced the other on the wall for support. It was the first time he'd seen the scars on his body from someone else's vantage point.

Before he could wrap his mind around the monster he'd become, the door opened. Surprised, Sidney nearly lost his balance but a strong set of arms reached out to steady him.

"What're you doing?" Nash asked.

"I needed to see."

Instead of scolding him for putting himself at risk, Nash lifted Sidney from the edge of the tub. "Come with me."

Nash led Sidney by the hand to the bedroom. In the corner of the small room was an antique oval floor mirror. He positioned Sidney in front of it. In that moment, Sidney realised he was standing naked in front of Nash. He moved one of his hands to shield his flaccid cock. It didn't matter that he'd been naked in front of Nash before. Sidney knew he wasn't the same person he'd been before the accident.

Nash met Sidney's gaze in the mirror. "What do you see when you look at yourself?"

Sidney openly studied his own reflection. "A skinny bald kid covered in stitches."

Nash kissed Sidney's neck. "Wanna know what I see?"

"We're looking in the same mirror, aren't we?"

"Evidently not. Because I see a miracle standing in front of me. Not the cuts or the short hair, just a big set of pretty green eyes looking back at me. Eyes that I was afraid I'd never again get the chance to gaze into and declare my love. You're a sexy son-of-a-bitch and don't ever think otherwise."

Sidney started to turn around, but Nash held him in place. Nash traced the row of stitches on Sidney's chest. "You had a damn good plastic surgeon. In a couple of years, you won't even know they're there."

I'll know, Sidney said to himself. *I'll always know.* Luke was still in a coma, and the doctors weren't overly optimistic he'd ever come out of it. Sidney felt the burn of tears. One kiss had ended any chance Luke could have of a normal life. Even if he woke from the coma, he would be paralysed and his brain wouldn't function the way it once had.

Before leaving the hospital, Sidney had talked to Maggie. He'd encouraged her to sue the insurance company for a large settlement. She'd seemed hesitant at first, but eventually agreed to discuss it with Alan. The Ballentines weren't the kind of people who would bring a law suit unless it was absolutely necessary, and from what Sidney had heard, Luke would need a lot of care if he survived.

"Sidney?" Nash prompted.

"Sorry. I was thinking about Luke." Sidney turned away from the mirror and stared up at Nash. "I guess you think I'm pretty selfish for thinking about myself when Luke's…" He shook his head, unable to continue.

Nash pulled Sidney into his arms. "I'm sorry about Luke, but I'm glad it wasn't you."

Sidney laid his good cheek on Nash's shoulder. The man was so incredibly sweet to him, but Sidney wasn't sure he deserved it. Still…who was he to look a gift horse in the mouth? "Of course you know what all these scars mean, don't you?" he asked in an effort to lighten the mood.

"What?"

"My dreams of being a high-priced stripper are over."

Nash began to chuckle. It was the sweetest sound Sidney had heard in months. Nash kissed the side of Sidney's head. "You can strip for me anytime."

* * * *

Nash pulled up in front of the barn and parked in his usual spot. He didn't see Jackson's truck in the drive, but he'd promised to give the man another day before he had to clear out of the house. Climbing out of the truck, he spotted Tommy and Steve working on the corral fence. "What happened? Looks like a tornado hit."

Tommy finished pounding in a nail before turning to face Nash. "Boss Man ran through it with his truck by accident."

Yeah, Nash just bet it was an accident. "When was that?"

"Yesterday. When he came by to check on Diablo," Steve answered.

Nash's spine stiffened. He'd long suspected it was Jackson who'd whipped the poor stallion, and the thought of the man being anywhere near the horse again didn't sit well at all. "He okay?"

"Jackson?" Tommy asked.

"Hell no. I meant Diablo," Nash clarified.

"The usual. You're the only one he lets near him, but we managed." Tommy pushed his cowboy hat out of his sightline and met Nash's stare. "What about the kid?"

Nash wasn't sure what to tell the ranch hands. He'd become so used to downplaying Sidney's injuries it was almost second nature to tell the guys Sidney was fine, but Nash knew better. Sooner or later they'd see Sidney. Nash decided it was better to prepare the men for that occasion rather than have Sidney see their shocked expressions.

Before he could get the words out, Tommy set his hammer

down and walked towards Nash. "That bad?"

Nash nodded. "He was lucky, don't get me wrong, but he's pretty cut up. The doctor who sewed him back together had to shave his head. He'll have a couple scars on his face, but one in particular is very noticeable despite the plastic surgeon's best efforts." Nash gestured to his torso and legs. "More hidden under his clothes."

"Damn," Tommy said.

"Yeah. If I can get him out of the house, try not to stare," Nash told the two men. Without another word, Nash strode towards the barn. He needed to check on Diablo for himself. It had been over a week since he'd seen the skittish stallion, and Nash had no idea what kind of set-back that would prove to be in Diablo's recovery.

"Hey, boy," he greeted.

Diablo snorted and took several steps back.

"I know you're pissed, but I had other things to deal with." Nash found the lawn chair he'd stashed by the stall. He unfolded the chair as slowly as he could before taking a seat. When Diablo still didn't approach the front of the stall, Nash reached down and grabbed two treats from the bucket beside him. He tossed one halfway between Diablo and the front, hoping to lure the horse forward.

Instead of going for the treat, Diablo moved back another step, putting himself in the corner. *Shit.* Nash sighed. One step forward and two steps back. He watched the skittish way Diablo moved and was reminded of Sidney. Not only did the two beautiful creatures believe their scars made them less than they were, but they both bore inner wounds that would be harder to heal.

Sidney still had nightmares; something Nash hoped would ease once the man was removed from the hospital setting. Nash couldn't imagine what it would be like to be kicked by the flailing legs of a dying deer, but it seemed to be more than that. Had Sidney seen Luke fly through the windshield? Had he heard the bones in Luke's back breaking, seen the impact that had done such permanent damage to the man's skull?

Nash closed his eyes and took a deep breath. As much as Nash would love to spend all his time with Diablo and Sidney, it simply wasn't possible. The men needed to be paid, which meant the books had to be brought up to date. It was the one aspect of Nash's job he hated. Maybe giving Sidney something to do while he recovered would be good for him. He wondered if it would do Sidney any good to sit with Diablo.

Even if Sidney was interested in spending time with the horse, Nash knew Sidney wasn't ready to expose his physical appearance to the other ranch hands.

Nash tossed the last treat into the stall before standing. "I'll be back later." *Baby steps.*

* * * *

Sidney was lying on the couch when Nash returned home for dinner. He'd been told to stay in bed, but the couch seemed less isolated. "Before you yell at me, you should know I put a sheet under me so I won't mess anything up."

Nash took off his boots and hat before walking towards Sidney. "I'd better check," he said with a grin on his face. He lifted the sheet covering Sidney's naked body. "Yep, you're telling the truth."

The heated expression on Nash's face as he stared down at him confused Sidney. Didn't the man see the roadmap of scars? As much as Sidney wanted to rip the sheet out of Nash's hand and cover himself, he found he quite liked Nash's attention. He let his legs fall open. "See something interesting down there?"

Nash brushed the back of his hand against Sidney's growing cock. Although they'd slept together the previous night, Sidney had shied away from Nash's touch. Nash repeated the movement. "I'll never be able to look at you without finding something interesting."

Sidney's groin was one of the few places on the front of his body that hadn't suffered damage. Maybe it was the reason Nash's attention didn't bother Sidney. As long as Nash's focus remained on the hard cock in his hand, he wouldn't notice the rest of Sidney's body as much.

Without a word, Nash dropped to his knees. He ran the tip of his tongue around the flared head of Sidney's cock before lapping at the slit dripping pre cum. Sidney's hips bucked at the attention.

Nash turned to stare into Sidney's eyes. "You up for this?"

Sidney ran a finger through the puddle of pre cum below his belly button. "What do you think?"

With a chuckle, Nash licked Sidney's cockhead before it dripped again. "I think I'm hungry."

Sidney rested his head against the pillow as warmth surrounded his cock. The swirl of Nash's tongue was almost his undoing. It had been a long time since someone had sucked him off, and since fucking wasn't possible for a few more days, Sidney would enjoy every ounce of Nash's attention.

He buried his fingers in Nash's hair. Usually, he enjoyed watching someone deep-throat his cock, but every time Sidney opened his eyes to stare down at Nash, all he could see were the rows of stitches. Even while being pleasured he couldn't release the reality of what had happened to him.

Sidney closed his eyes and tried to block out everything but the feel of Nash's throat as it worked his cock. Damn, the man knew how to give a blowjob. A spit-laced finger found its way to Sidney's hole and gently probed.

With a moan, Sidney thrust up, wincing as the stitches reminded him, once again, of his predicament. He couldn't wait to heal, to feel Nash's length slamming into him. Sidney gasped when Nash's finger prodded his prostate. "So good."

Nash scraped his teeth against the thin skin of Sidney's cock, sending Sidney over the edge. Sidney's cry of ecstasy came out more like a woman's scream, but he was too immersed in riding out his orgasm to care.

Only when the last shot of cum left his cock did Sidney open his eyes. He stared down at Nash. It was then he spotted Nash's free hand jerking away on his own cock. "Here." He opened his mouth as far as he could without hurting himself and stuck out his tongue, hoping Nash would feed him as well.

Nash released Sidney's spent cock. "You want some of this?" he asked, getting to his feet.

"Hell yeah." Sidney licked his lips as he watched Nash slide his hand up and down the length of the long, fat cock.

Nash wiped the tip of his cock against Sidney's tongue, depositing a tasty strand of pre cum. "Sexy," Nash said when Sidney began rubbing his tongue along the underside of Nash's cock.

"More." Sidney opened his mouth again and gazed up into Nash's eyes. He watched the changing expressions on Nash's face as the handsome man shot his first load. The splash of thick cum only partially made it to Sidney's mouth with the remainder painting Sidney's lip and cheek.

Nash's second volley found its mark, coating Sidney's tongue. Fuck, Nash tasted good. Sidney pulled Nash closer before wrapping his lips around the spent cock. He cleaned Nash thoroughly before releasing the flaccid organ. "Better than anything either of us can make in the kitchen," he said with a grin.

Nash tucked himself back into his underwear before kneeling beside the sofa. He swiped the cum from Sidney's cheek with his tongue before sharing a deep kiss. Breaking the lip lock, Nash chuckled. "Just wait until you're well. I bet I can make something equally good in the kitchen if I put my mind to it." He kissed the tip of Sidney's nose. "Ever been fucked in the kitchen?"

Sidney shook his head. "Not many kitchens in the places I'm used to getting action."

"Then you're in for a treat." Nash pulled the sheet up over Sidney. He began massaging Sidney's spent cock. "I'm not sure how long I'll get you to stay here, but I don't plan to waste a second of the time we have together, so prepare yourself."

The thought of being taken by Nash day and night had been his biggest fantasy. "I'm not going anywhere," Sidney told Nash. How could he when he finally had a real chance with the one person he'd always wanted?

"Sure you will, but you're here for now." Nash gave Sidney a quick kiss. "And like I said, I don't plan on wasting our time together."

Arguing with Nash wouldn't do any good, so Sidney let the subject of his leaving drop. "What about your teacher? Still plan on seeing him?"

"Of course not."

Sidney's stomach growled, interrupting their conversation. Just as well because Sidney didn't want to dwell on Nash's arrangement with Reece. "I made some vegetable beef soup earlier today. I don't suppose I could talk you into reheating it for us?"

"What were you doing up making soup?" Nash asked.

"Don't get too excited. I used canned vegetables, so the only thing I had to do was brown the stew meat and throw it all together."

Nash sighed and ran his finger under Sidney's chin. "You should just concentrate on getting better. Believe me, I need you to get better." Nash moved his hand back down Sidney's body to squeeze his cock, leaving Sidney with no doubt as to what he really needed.

"I'm sure we could come up with a comfortable position to fuck if we put our minds to it." Sidney ran the back of his hand across the front of Nash's underwear when he stood.

Nash grunted at the contact. "I think I can control myself for another couple of days."

Sidney turned his hand over and cupped the heavy sac that sat prominently in Nash's white briefs. "Maybe I can't."

Nash used his hand to press Sidney's palm more firmly against his awakening cock. "Try and control yourself, because the last thing I want is to hurt you in any way." He released his hold on Sidney's hand and stepped back, out of Sidney's reach. "I'll go get dinner ready. You up to sitting at the table?"

"Sure," Sidney answered. He waited until Nash walked into the kitchen before throwing the sheet off. He winced as he sat up. It was the long, healing wound on his stomach that seemed to give him the most trouble. Although the laceration hadn't done any damage to his organs, the muscle had been sliced through. He still couldn't figure out how the dying deer had managed to do so much damage. It was still all a blur. He remembered the events but it had all seemed to happen so fast he still couldn't pinpoint when each injury had occurred.

Sidney put his hand to the wound on his lower left side and sat up, wincing as he did. The nurse in the hospital had chuckled when he'd complained about the injury. She told him there was an entire wing of C-section patients who were busy complaining about the same thing. It wasn't the first time he'd been compared to a woman and surely it wouldn't be the last. What he couldn't figure out was why a woman would suffer the kind of pain he was in and elect to do it again. No wonder he preferred dick to pussy. Women were just weird.

Chapter Eight

"Do you feel like moving back into the main house today?" Nash asked while pulling on his socks.

"What about you?" Sidney ran a hand down Nash's spine. "Are you sick of me already?"

Nash turned to face Sidney. It had been a week since Jackson had left the ranch, but every time Nash brought up moving, Sidney shut him down. Although they were trying to take things slowly, both sexually and emotionally, Nash was completely addicted to everything Sidney had to offer.

"What in the world would give you that idea?" Nash ran his hand up Sidney's thigh. The last of the stitches had been removed two days before, and the healing skin was still pinkish-brown. "I was kind of hoping you'd invite me to stay a while."

"You'd do that?"

"In a heartbeat." Nash's touch wandered to Sidney's cock. He wished he had time for another round with the sexy man, but it was already going on seven o' clock and chores needed to be done.

"I'd be able to see you more if we lived there, right?" Sidney moved to rub the heel of his foot against the growing bulge in Nash's jeans.

"Damn straight. Although it could also get us into trouble." The thought of slipping away to the house for a quick fuck would be a hell of a temptation.

"Who's it going to get you into trouble with? No way I'm gonna complain."

Nash knew it was the right time to bring up his plan for Sidney. "If we're living that close to the barn, I wonder if you could help me out with something."

Sidney's head rolled to the side. The younger man had made it pretty clear he hated ranch work. "Go on."

"I don't have the time to give Diablo the attention he needs. I was hoping I could get you to spend a couple hours a day sitting with him."

"Have you forgotten that he tried to smash my face in with his hooves? I don't think he likes me much."

Nash shook his head. He moved his touch down to brush back and forth across Sidney's balls. "I think the biggest thing Diablo needs is someone to trust. I was doing a pretty decent job before you lured me into your bed. Now I don't have the free time I used to have."

"And you really just want me to sit there?" Sidney asked.

"That's it." Although Nash didn't say it, he hoped the situation would help both man and horse. Besides, it would give Sidney something to do besides dwelling on Luke and the accident.

Maggie had phoned the previous night to inform Sidney of their plans to move Luke to a rehabilitation hospital as soon as he was strong enough. The doctors were still taking a wait-and-see attitude towards Luke's chance of recovery.

"Okay," Sidney eventually agreed. "On one condition."

Nash rolled his eyes. Sidney had done the 'one condition' thing since he'd known him. "What's that?"

"You help me set up a drafting table in the barn. If I'm gonna spend hours out there, I might as well do something constructive with my time."

"Deal."

* * * *

Nash carried Sidney's suitcases upstairs and stopped. "Should I put these in your old room or the master bedroom?"

"My room," Sidney answered, slowly making his way up the stairs. The thought of sleeping in his dad's bed sent shivers up Sidney's spine. He noticed Nash giving him that look again. Sidney couldn't put his finger on it, but it was almost as if Nash was waiting for Sidney to break or something. "My room has the best view of the barn," he said, hoping to set Nash's mind at ease.

"Okay." Nash continued down the hall to the back of the house. "On the bed?"

"Yeah, that's fine." Sidney entered his room and looked around. His gaze landed on his mom's worn leather hat, Old Ben, that hung on the wall. Suddenly, he longed to be surrounded by his mom's things. He briefly wondered if he'd find more treasures of hers hidden in the master bedroom.

"Something wrong?" Nash asked, reaching for Sidney's hand.

"Not really. But I think I'd like some time alone." He gestured to the suitcases. "Ya know, to get settled in again."

Nash lifted Sidney's hand to his lips and kissed the palm. "Sure. Just ring the dinner bell on the porch if you need me."

"Thanks." Sidney stood on his tiptoes and gave Nash a quick kiss. The man had been incredibly understanding with Sidney's mood swings.

Nash pulled away and left the room. Sidney heard Nash's boots on the hardwood floor as he walked down the hall. The sound stopped for a moment before continuing. Nash was obviously reluctant to leave Sidney alone, but why?

As soon as Sidney heard the front door close, he walked across the room and lifted Old Ben from its hook. The leather felt stiff and dry, something his mother would've never stood for. Despite its condition, Sidney carried it to the mirror before putting it on.

Although it was a woman's hat, Old Ben fit Sidney's bald head perfectly. He promised himself he'd get something from the barn to help bring the dark leather back to life. Satisfied, he took off the hat and laid it on his dresser.

It was then he spotted the bottle of White Shoulders

perfume. Had Nash bought it in town and put it there? Sidney went to the closet and pulled his mom's pink sweater off the hanger. Clutched in his hands, Sidney lifted the garment to his face. He closed his eyes as he inhaled the smell of his mom. Sidney knew smell prompted memories, and one came immediately to mind.

It was just days before his mom's death. He remembered coming home from school and going straight to her bedroom. In the big King-sized bed, his emaciated mother had looked so incredibly small in her nightgown and pink sweater.

Sidney swallowed around the lump in his throat. He didn't like to remember his mom that way. Before the cancer she'd been a strong, loving woman who would've done anything for Sidney. How many times had his mother talked to him about the importance of keeping the Running E in their family?

With a heavy sigh, Sidney sat on the window seat and gazed out over the land his mom had loved so much. What would happen to it once he was gone? It was the first time in his life Sidney had wished he was straight. Knowing he didn't want a life on the ranch only made things worse. What if he left and his dad tried to move back in?

Thoughts of his dad brought up more painful truths. Sidney needed to see a copy of the will, and he knew it would be pointless to look for one in the house. It was up to him to make sure there were no loopholes his dad could slip through to claim possession of the Running E.

Before he knew it, Sidney was standing outside the barn with Old Ben covering his head. It was the first time he'd come anywhere near the men who worked the Running E since the accident. Although the men had always been nice to him, Sidney didn't know any of them well, except Nash, of course, but Nash had always been different.

He entered the barn. "Nash?"

A head popped up from within one of the stalls. It was a younger man Sidney didn't recognise. "Can I help you?"

Sidney took a step towards the man. "I'm Sidney Wilks." He continued forwards and held his hand over the stall.

"Lonnie," the young man introduced himself and shook Sidney's hand.

"I'm looking for Nash."

"He just got a call. I think he went out back to take it."

Sidney nodded. "Thanks." As he walked off, Sidney couldn't help but wonder what Lonnie thought of him. Although the man hadn't stared at the scars on Sidney's face, there was no doubt he'd noticed them.

Doesn't matter, Sidney told himself. The wide double doors used to transfer the horses in and out of the barn were open, and the phone cord was stretched around the corner. He started to step outside, but something Nash said stopped him in his tracks.

"I'm sorry, Reece. I know I should've called."

The name of Nash's other lover hit Sidney like a two by four between the eyes. He wanted to run out and tell Nash to end the call, but couldn't make himself take a single step.

"Yeah," Nash continued. "Okay, I'll meet you at Gregory's at eight."

Sidney was still standing just inside the barn when Nash almost ran into him. "Hey." Nash brushed Sidney's cheek with his hand before hanging the phone back on its hook. He grinned down at Sidney. "The hat looks good."

Sidney shrugged. Was Nash going to pretend he wasn't just on the phone making a date with another man? "It needs to be conditioned," he managed to say.

"I see that. Why don't you leave it with me, and I'll get it all fixed up for you?"

Sidney took off the hat and held it out without saying a word.

"Something wrong?" Nash asked, taking Old Ben.

"You going out tonight?" Sidney got up the nerve to ask. A picture of Nash wearing his tightest jeans and sexy black cowboy hat came to mind.

Nash's eyes widened momentarily. He surprised Sidney

with a crooked grin. "You heard that, did ya?"

"Yep." Sidney waited. Nash had never lied to him, but there was always a first time.

Strong arms wrapped around Sidney. "It's not what you think, so get those thoughts right out of this pretty head of yours."

"I heard you make a date. So tell me exactly what I'm supposed to think?" Sidney couldn't bring himself to look Nash in the eyes.

"I don't know. Maybe that Reece has been a friend for too damn long to just end things over the phone? That he deserves to actually hear that I'm in love with someone else face-to-face instead of through a text message?" Nash released his hold on Sidney and took a step back. "I won't cheat on you. Not ever. Either you believe that or you don't. This is one of the reasons I fought my feelings for you. I still don't know how the hell a relationship between us is gonna work, but one thing is for certain. You're finishing that degree of yours, which means you'll be leaving at the end of summer. Now, you can choose to make yourself miserable by worrying that I'm out fucking someone else, or you can concentrate on your studies knowing I love you. The choice is yours."

Before Sidney could say a word, Nash walked out of the barn, Old Ben still clutched in his hand. Sidney wanted to run after Nash, but he couldn't. Despite what Nash said, Sidney knew he would always worry. Nash may not be a cheater, but that didn't mean he wouldn't find someone and break up with Sidney before making a move on the other guy.

"Did you find him?" Lonnie asked, pushing a wheelbarrow full of straw and crap towards Sidney.

"Yeah," Sidney answered. He watched as Lonnie's gaze swept over the scars now visible on Sidney's bare head. Suddenly, Sidney needed to get away. Driving himself to the Reno County Courthouse in Hutchinson was impossible, but he could put off getting a copy of the will for another day or so. Still, he needed a place to think.

Sidney thought about just taking off for the afternoon, but he knew he couldn't do that either. Before Lonnie left the barn, Sidney called out, "If anyone needs me I'll be at the cemetery."

* * * *

Nash pulled along the side of the road and parked behind the ranch truck in front of the Running Elk family cemetery. The stacked-stone wall surrounding the one acre resting place always amazed Nash. The wall had been constructed over a hundred years earlier and not a stone was out of place.

He spotted Sidney on a blanket under the old walnut tree that shaded his mother's grave. Nash remembered the fit Jackson had thrown at burying his wife in that particular location. Jackson hadn't liked the idea of the tree's roots eventually destroying Elizabeth's casket. Elizabeth had just shaken her head and tried to explain to her grieving husband that by becoming part of the tree, she would live on for years to come.

"Hey," Nash greeted. "Lonnie told me you were out here." Nash sat on the corner of the blanket and rested his back against the tree. He took off his cowboy hat and set it on the grass.

Sidney's eyes remained closed, but Nash knew the younger man wasn't asleep. "I can feel her here."

"I know." Nash had found a distraught Sidney at his mom's grave on more than one occasion over the years. There were no doubts in Nash's mind as to why Sidney was currently seeking the comfort of his mom. The conversation in the barn hadn't gone well. Nash knew he sounded harsher than he'd meant to, but at the time he couldn't believe Sidney would question his loyalty. It wasn't until after he'd walked away that he realised why Sidney would worry.

"I've known Reece for almost eight years. Been fucking him for about the same amount of time," Nash began.

"I don't think I want to hear this," Sidney mumbled.

"I'm sure you don't, but you didn't let me finish. What I was going to tell you is that I've fucked Reece for the last eight years and never once felt it was anything more than a fuck. One night with you and I knew what making love was all about. It sounds corny as hell, but I can't go back. You've got me."

Sidney finally opened his eyes and turned his head towards Nash. "Is he handsome?"

"Yes." Nash moved to stretch out beside Sidney. He traced a few of the small, dark scars on Sidney's head. "But so are you." He ran his hand over the small amount of black fuzz. "I know you don't think so, but I have a feeling you're not really seeing yourself anymore. I think you're seeing the face of a man who was driving a car when a friend's life was changed forever."

Sidney quickly turned away, dislodging Nash's hand. "Of course I am. How could I not when I'm faced with what I did every fucking time I look into a mirror?"

"I wish I could wave a magic wand and take away your guilt, but I can't. And I won't tell you not to feel what you're feeling, because I'm sure I'd be going through the exact same emotions if our positions were reversed. But you *will* get through this. *We* will get through this." Nash laid a hand on the centre of Sidney's chest.

Sidney met Nash's gaze with tears in his eyes. "I kissed Luke."

The confession made Nash feel uneasy. "Is that all you did with him?"

Sidney shook his head as if he were frustrated. "It's not the kiss. The kiss didn't mean anything."

"So what did?" Nash asked, confused.

"He unbuckled himself so he could kiss me while I was driving that night."

The impact of the statement took Nash aback for a

moment. He just laid there and stared at Sidney.

"Now do you understand? I think Josh knows. I think that's why he can't stand to look at or talk to me."

Nash scooted closer to Sidney before pulling the man into his arms. Although he understood Sidney's guilt, Nash knew he wasn't alone. "If you're guilty, so am I. I shouldn't have pushed you away like I did. Maybe if I hadn't the kiss would've never happened. And unless you unbuckled Luke's seatbelt, he shares some of the blame as well."

With his injured cheek resting against Nash's chest, Sidney squeezed Nash tighter. "I love you."

"I love you, too." Nash thought of his meeting with Reece. Although it was important he speak to Reece in person, he couldn't bring himself to leave Sidney for the evening. "I'll call Reece and tell him I can't make it tonight."

"You don't have to," Sidney mumbled.

"Yeah, I do. He has an idea of what's going on anyway, so I'm sure he'll understand if I need to reschedule."

Sidney moved to rest his chin on Nash's chest. "I need to go into Hutch sometime to get a copy of my mom's will. Maybe the two of you can have a drink or something together while I do that."

Nash looked at the sky through the tree branches. Was Sidney trying to compromise, or was he simply hoping to control the amount of time Nash spent with Reece? Did it matter? Nash only needed to talk to Reece for long enough to end things respectfully. "Sounds good," he finally said.

Sidney scooted up until they were face to face. "Will you see him again once I go back to school?"

Staring into Sidney's big green eyes, Nash couldn't imagine anyone else taking his place. "No." In his heart, he knew he was condemning himself to a life of loneliness. Although Sidney would return to the ranch from time to time, Nash would never have the domestic life he'd always secretly desired.

Sidney smiled. The fresh scar might fade, but Sidney's smile had been forever altered. Instead of the big boyish smile Nash had come to love, the scar prevented Sidney's lips on one side from stretching fully, creating a more rakish grin. Nash thought the scar made Sidney even sexier than he already was. He pulled Sidney's head down for a deep kiss.

Without thinking, Nash rolled over on top of Sidney. He broke the kiss and stared down at the man who owned his heart. "Am I hurting you?"

"Never," Sidney answered before thrusting his tongue into Nash's mouth.

Nash braced himself on his forearms, hoping to keep most of his weight off Sidney's still-healing torso. The direct contact of his cock to Sidney's was what he needed. He ground against Sidney's erection, wishing he'd brought lube. He could easily get both of them off without fucking, but Nash wanted to hear Sidney get loud, something he only seemed to do while being ridden hard.

With a groan, Nash broke the kiss. "We need to go home. Now." He adjusted the erection trapped in his jeans after standing. Nash held out his hand. "Will you follow me?"

Sidney let Nash help him to his feet. "I'll be right behind you. Just need to say a quick goodbye."

Nash held the back of Sidney's head in place as he plundered the sexy mouth once more with his tongue. "Hurry. I'm about to go off in my jeans."

"Well then, I guess you'd better get home and take them off." Sidney pressed his body against Nash's cock. "Grab the blanket."

Nash pulled away before scooping the blanket up off the ground. He watched as Sidney bent to place a kiss on Elizabeth's headstone. He couldn't hear what Sidney whispered to the black granite, but when he stood, he looked more at peace.

They headed out of the cemetery hand in hand. Nash helped Sidney into the large farm truck. "I've got to stop by my place for a second, but I'll be at the ranch in a few."

Nash needed to call Reece, but doing it from Sidney's

house seemed disrespectful. He parked in his driveway before running inside. He needed to make it quick.

"Hey," Reece answered. "I was just getting ready to jump in the shower."

"I'm glad I caught you in time then. Sorry, something's come up and I need to cancel, but I was hoping you could meet me for lunch tomorrow."

"Lunch? I don't know. Maybe." Reece sighed. "It's over, isn't it?"

"Yeah," Nash confirmed. "But that doesn't mean we can't still be friends."

Reece was quiet for several moments, and Nash was afraid of what was coming. "Look," Reece began. "We don't need to have lunch."

"Are you saying you don't want to even be friends?" Nash asked. Even though he knew he could never fall in love with Reece, he was still a fun guy to talk to.

"Give it some time."

"Yeah, okay." Nash winced at the hurt he detected in Reece's voice. Their relationship had just been about fucking, right? Nash wondered if it had changed for Reece somewhere along the line. Although he hated himself for causing pain to his friend, Nash had never promised anything more than a few hours of mutual satisfaction.

The call ended without either of them saying goodbye. Maybe it was better that way. Nash hung up the phone before heading back to his truck. He'd done the right thing, the only thing, so why did he feel like a piece of shit for doing it?

The short drive to the ranch house cooled his ardour but not his love.

Reaching the ranch, he climbed out of the truck and watched Sidney emerge from the equipment barn. The sight of Sidney's lean body silhouetted against the setting sun drove all thoughts of Reece from Nash's mind. The man walking towards him was worth giving up everything for.

Chapter Nine

Sidney handed Nash a glass of iced tea to go with his big plate of spaghetti before sitting down to eat. The two of them had gone into the courthouse earlier that day, and Sidney had been able to get a copy of his mother's will. For some inane reason, Sidney had believed the will would give him answers, not pose more questions. "Can I ask you something that might seem kinda nosy?"

Nash took a drink and wiped his mouth on the back of his hand. "Sure."

"How much rent did you pay Dad?"

"One-fifty a month. Why?"

Sidney held out the copy of the will. "According to this, he wasn't supposed to charge you anything."

"Fucker," Nash grumbled before taking a bite of spaghetti.

"I'll make sure you get it back. All of it," Sidney added.

"Not necessary."

"Sure it is." Sidney fingered a corner of the small stack of papers. He'd already discussed with Nash the provision in the will that forbade selling the land, but they hadn't talked about what he'd do with it. "So, I was wondering if you'd completely take over the ranch for me?" he finally asked.

Nash set down his fork and took another drink of his tea before answering. "What do you mean?"

Sidney laid his napkin on the table before getting to his feet. He stood beside Nash until his hunky cowboy got the hint and scooted his chair back so Sidney could sit on his lap. "We both know I don't want to run this ranch. If you weren't here, I'd sell off every damn head of cattle and let the land go back to its natural state."

"And you'd put a few good men out of work," Nash reminded him.

"I know, which is why I'm asking you to make a trade with me." Sidney began to pepper soft kisses on Nash's face and neck.

Nash's hands began squeezing Sidney's butt. "You want me to work the ranch in exchange for sex?"

With a chuckle, Sidney shook his head. "Naw, you can have the sex for free. I want to trade you the money I figure the ranch owes you for the rent you paid in exchange for all the livestock and equipment."

Nash's hands stilled. "Why would you do that?"

"Because it's the best way I know to keep you here. And I want you to have a stake in this place because you've more than earned it over the years. The only thing I ask is enough profit to pay the taxes."

"I can't do that. The Running E is your inheritance," Nash started to argue.

"The land is what was important to my mom, not the ranch." He gave Nash a deep kiss. He'd done a lot of thinking and certain things were beginning to add up. "There must've been a reason my mom wanted you to live in my grandfather's house. Did she know you were gay?"

"I don't know. If she did she never said anything." Nash reached between them and popped the button at the top of Sidney's jeans. He insinuated his hand down the back of Sidney's jeans to tickle the top of his crack. "Even if she knew, I doubt it would've prompted her to make sure I had a place to live."

The finger sliding up and down the crack of his ass nearly caused Sidney to lose focus. "She wanted you in my life." Sidney stood and began removing his clothes. "I want you in my life," he said, moving in the direction of the living room.

"Where the hell are you going?" Nash called when Sidney left the room.

"To watch television. You go ahead and finish your

dinner." Sidney grabbed the box of condoms and small bottle of lube from the table in the foyer where he'd stashed them earlier.

"The hell I will." Nash's chair scraped against the kitchen floor moments before he appeared. His eyes opened wide as he studied the living room. "Been planning have ya?"

Sidney stretched out on the pallet of blankets before reaching for the remote. "It gets better. Look what came in the mail today." He pushed the play button on the VHS player and the twenty-five inch console television began to show a scene of two men fucking in a barn.

"Holy fuck," Nash said, removing his clothes.

When Sidney had discovered Nash had never watched a porn movie, he'd immediately gone to the back of one of his favourite fuck magazines and ordered quite a collection. "This one's called *Deep and Hard in Texas*. I thought it might give you some good ideas."

Nash couldn't seem to take his eyes off the screen. He stumbled to the blankets and almost fell on top of Sidney. "Shit. Sorry."

Sidney decided to take pity on Nash and let him continue to watch the cowboy getting fucked over a saw horse. He crawled between Nash's legs and buried his face in the short dark hair surrounding Nash's rock hard cock.

Nash grunted at the first swipe of Sidney's tongue up the length of his cock.

"You gonna fuck me like that someday?" Sidney asked, running his tongue around the head of Nash's cock.

"Mmm hmm." Nash's hand landed on the top of Sidney's head. "I don't think those guys are real cowboys," Nash said.

Sidney released the dick in his mouth before looking up at Nash. "Why do you say that?"

"Look at those boots. I bet those cost at least five hundred bucks."

Sidney reached for the bottle of lube. "Really? That's what you're focussing on? You mean the fact that his ass is as brown as the rest of him didn't clue you in? Or that he supposedly just came in off the range in a pair of chaps and nothing else?"

"That could happen," Nash chuckled.

Sidney licked his lips. Nash's Christmas chaps had come in a few days earlier and although Nash had tried them on and showed them off right away, he'd been wearing jeans underneath. "You telling me you'd play that game with me?"

"Maybe if I knew I wouldn't get caught." Nash squirted some lube onto his hand. He continued to watch the cowboys fuck as he began to slick Sidney's hole.

Sidney stuck his ass in the air and let Nash play while he turned his attention to the movie. He tried to picture Nash in a pair of chaps and nothing else. Fuck. He'd come on the spot. "I think that saw horse would give you splinters."

Nash removed his fingers from Sidney's hole and replaced them with his cock. He sank in to the hilt and bent over to rest his chest against Sidney's back. "I'll throw a horse blanket over the one in the barn for ya, babe."

It was the first time Nash had used a term of endearment, and Sidney found he quite enjoyed it. Suddenly he wanted to be fucked face-to-face. "I wanna look at you. Screw the TV, I wanna watch *my* cowboy."

With the sound of two men fucking in the background, Nash withdrew. "Should I put the movie on pause?"

Sidney chuckled and rolled to his back. "We can watch it again if we miss something."

Sitting on his heels, Nash stared down at Sidney. "Are you sure you're okay to do it this way?"

Sidney hooked his forearms under his knees and brought his legs up against his chest. There was a slight pull to the healing areas, but nothing that felt risky. "I'm good."

Nash circled Sidney's stretched hole with the tip of his finger. "You certainly are."

Rolling his eyes, Sidney blew Nash a kiss. "Fuck me, cowboy."

Insinuating himself against Sidney's exposed hole, Nash thrust his cock deep into Sidney's body.

"Yes," Sidney cried. "Fuck that ass," he said, mimicking the cowboy on TV.

Nash grabbed Sidney's ankles. "Squeeze me."

Doing as instructed, Sidney did his best to wrap his legs around Nash's back. There was really no hope of being able to cross his ankles to hold him there, but he gave it his best shot. The new position allowed Nash to lie on top of Sidney.

Sidney tried for several moments to chase Nash's mouth with his own. He wanted a kiss but the man seemed so intent on watching the movie and fucking Sidney's brains out that he wouldn't keep his head still long enough for Sidney to latch on. "Kiss me, dammit!"

Nash blinked and glanced down at Sidney. "Don't bring this shit home if you don't want me to watch it."

"It's supposed to get you in the mood, not take over," Sidney argued, although there was no heat in his voice. Knowing Nash was getting into the movie thrilled Sidney. He'd watched porn at a gross movie theatre in Pennsylvania, but he'd never thought there'd come a day when someone else would enjoy watching it with him.

Nash smashed his mouth against Sidney's and thrust his tongue inside. Sidney whimpered into the kiss as Nash's cock hammered in and out of him. He couldn't wait for his body to completely heal so he could beg Nash to fuck him even harder, but with each thrust, Sidney felt a slight twinge of pain in his stomach wound. Of course he'd keep his mouth shut. Telling Nash his fucking hurt where it wasn't supposed to would only end Sidney's fun.

The fake cowboys on the screen were still going at it when Nash broke the kiss. "I thought I'd try to outlast them, but it's not going to happen," Nash panted.

Sidney opened his mouth to reply just as a hand wrapped around his cock. His mouth opened and an incoherent string of words flew out. "Motherfucker. Good. Too good," he babbled as the first strand of cum jetted from his cock.

Nash pounded deep inside Sidney's ass a few more times before he howled Sidney's name.

Sidney held on to Nash as his lover's body shook with the intensity of his climax. Several minutes later, Nash shook his head where it rested beside Sidney's. "And they're still going."

It took Sidney a second to figure out what Nash was talking about, but when the men on the TV began to really get loud, he laughed. "Their asses are probably numb after all the filming."

Nash rolled to the side, pulling out of Sidney. "Good to know. At least I don't feel like such a failure now." He rolled to the side and pulled Sidney into his arms.

Sidney snuggled against Nash's broad chest. "Far from it." He swiped Nash's nipple with his tongue. Closing his eyes, he sighed in contentment. "I could fall asleep right here," he mumbled.

Nash chuckled. "I wish I could, but I've still got dinner to finish and a ranch to lock down for the night."

Sidney sighed again, but this time it wasn't out of contentment. Would the damn ranch always be an interruption?

* * * *

Nash groaned in ecstasy as the cold water from the hose served to both clean and cool him. He hated hay season, but it was a necessary evil. Glancing at his hands, he winced. It would take a good hour of digging with a needle to get all the slivers of hay out of his hands, but gloves made the job go even slower, in his opinion.

Entering the barn, he spotted Sidney at his drafting table outside Diablo's stall. After the stallion's reaction to the pasture the previous day, Nash began to worry there was no hope for a recovery. "Hey," he greeted.

Sidney glanced up from his design and smiled. "Mmm, hot sweaty cowboy. My favourite kind."

Nash bent and gave Sidney a deep kiss. Pulling back, he realised he'd dripped on the large sheet of paper. "Oh shit, I'm sorry."

With a swipe of his hand, Sidney rid the design of most of the water. "It's okay. This one's just for me."

Nash leaned a hand against the edge of the table and studied the sketch. He shook his head at the amazing skill evident in every straight line and curve of the building. Sidney definitely had a style all of his own. "I've never seen anything like it."

"That's the idea. Although I haven't quite figured out all the engineering involved, I like the concept." Sidney chuckled. "Guess that's why I should get my ass back to school."

The mention of school soured Nash's mood immediately. He knew the time was coming, but he wasn't ready to say goodbye yet.

"What's wrong?" Sidney asked.

"Nothin'," Nash mumbled.

Sidney opened the long, thin drawer that ran the width of his table and pulled out a brochure. He tossed it onto the table with a big, lopsided grin. "Look at this, and tell me what you think?"

The words K-State jumped out at Nash from the front of the coloured cover. "You thinking about changing schools?" He held his breath. It was more than he could've hoped for.

"Not thinking about it. I did it. I applied, got accepted and start in August. I'll lose a few credit hours, but if I take classes in the summer, I should still be able to graduate in five years." Sidney reached out and grabbed Nash's hand. "It's less than two hours from here. I can even commute if I want."

The thought of Sidney driving four hours a day wasn't an option as far as Nash was concerned. "You'd do better to stay in town during the week and come home on weekends. At least that would give you more time to study."

"Yeah, you're probably right. Maybe I can schedule my

classes for four days a week. At least that would give me longer weekends."

At least with Sidney transferring colleges, Nash would get another few years with him. He couldn't seem to wipe the smile off his face.

"You like that idea, do ya?" Sidney asked around a laugh.

"Definitely." Nash leant down to give Sidney another deep kiss. He heard the loud roar of the loaded hay truck pull up outside the barn and broke the kiss. "We'll have to celebrate later. Right now I need to help the guys unload."

Before leaving, Nash gestured to Diablo. Like every day, Diablo stood in the back corner of his stall. "How's he doing today?"

"The same." Sidney went to stand in front of the stall. "What do you think really happened to him?"

Nash joined Sidney with an arm around his waist. "I don't know. I mean, it's obvious someone whipped him, but the why or the who won't change anything." He decided to voice his biggest worry in regards to the once-beautiful stallion. "Maybe it would be better to put him down."

"Kill him?"

Nash knew the idea of putting an animal to sleep would upset Sidney, but he needed to face the realities of ranch life. "Look at him, babe. He's afraid of his own shadow. When we put him outside yesterday he jumped the damn fence trying to get away from the other horses." Nash kissed the soft, short hair on the top of Sidney's head. "I just worry we're doing more harm than good."

Sidney squared his shoulders. "I won't let you put him down while there's still a chance he'll come out of it."

Nash wondered if Sidney's reaction had anything to do with Luke. Although Luke was still in a coma, the Ballentine family refused to give up hope. "Okay, we'll take it a day at a time."

* * * *

127

At the tail end of his two hour drive home, Sidney thought back upon the disagreement he'd had with one of his professors. Although Professor Adams had complimented Sidney on the aesthetic aspects of his design, he'd informed Sidney it wasn't buildable.

Sidney refused to take Adams' statement as fact. He'd figure out a way to make the curves and angles stable enough to build if he had to spend the rest of his life doing it. The idea for the building had come to him one evening while waiting for Nash to come in from the northwest pasture. Sidney had been fascinated by the way the grass, bushes and trees blew in the stronger than usual wind. The movement itself stirred something inside him he couldn't explain.

Used to designing buildings in the traditional style with his own added twists, Sidney began to wonder what would happen if he threw out the rule book and drew something no one had ever seen before. What if a building didn't have to look like a building at all? What if he took ideas from nature and designed buildings that truly fit in with their surroundings?

He glanced at the tube in the passenger seat that held countless hours of work. Sidney's design was unusual, he already knew that much. With a façade of graduating shades of blue and clear glass, the structure looked more like a cresting wave than an office building.

His brand new brick phone rang, startling him out of his train of thought. He reached down and turned off the Journey cassette he'd been listening to before grabbing the phone. Although incredibly expensive, Nash had been the one to talk Sidney into buying it. It had been over a year since the accident, but Nash still worried every time Sidney made the two hour trek to and from Manhattan. "Hello?"

"Hey. Just thought I'd see how far out you are," Nash said.

"About fifteen minutes give or take. Why, what's up?"

"I've got Diablo out in the pasture, and I think there's something you need to see."

Sidney's heart skipped a beat. He'd spent almost every weekend working with the scarred stallion. The thought of something happening to the timid sweetheart scared him to death. "Is he okay?"

"More than. You'll see when you get here. Drive safe."

"I will." Sidney pushed the button, ending the call. He wondered why Nash had Diablo out of his stall in such crappy weather. The closer he got to home, the heavier it seemed to rain. *Great.* The ranch yard would be nothing but a pit of mud, which was typical for October in Kansas, but sucked anyway.

By the time he reached home, it was pouring rain. Instead of heading to the house, he drove towards the barn. Sidney parked his SUV before making a mad dash to the man waiting just inside the open door. "Man, it's coming down," he said, flying into Nash's arms, knocking off his cowboy's hat in the process.

"Been raining like this most of the day." Nash bent over and picked up his hat, with an arm still wrapped around Sidney. After resettling his hat, he took Sidney's mouth in a passionate kiss.

Sidney opened to the exploring tongue. How many times had Nash kissed him over the last year? Not enough was the immediate answer that came to mind. Sidney knew he'd never tire of his big cowboy. Coming up for air, Sidney stared at Nash. "Show me."

Those big brown eyes rounded. "Right here?"

Laughing, Sidney kissed Nash again. "Not that, although I'm sure I'll need to inspect every inch of your body later, I was talking about Diablo."

"Oh." Nash shrugged. "I guess if you don't want it now…"

"Stop." Sidney reached out and physically turned Nash towards the back of the barn. "Now show me."

Nash reached back and grabbed Sidney's hand as he strode to the door. "I made a mistake this morning when I put him out. I thought Buckwheat was with the mares, but evidently he'd got into the west pasture."

Sidney skidded to a stop. No matter how hard they tried, Diablo refused to be around other horses without going batshit crazy. Having the sweet-tempered buckskin gelding in the same pasture with Diablo could be disastrous. "Please tell me they're both okay?"

Nash yanked Sidney forwards. Once they reached the doorway, Nash took a pair of binoculars off the hook beside the door before handing them to Sidney. "See for yourself."

Sidney could see a blob of colour in the back of the pasture. Focusing in, Sidney's mouth dropped open. "Oh my God." The two male horses were nuzzling each other like a couple of newlyweds.

"Yeah," Nash agreed. "You should've seen my face earlier when I caught sight of Diablo mounting Buckwheat and Buckwheat just standing there letting him."

Sidney lowered the binoculars and turned to face Nash. "Are you telling me that horse is gay?"

Nash nodded. "I called Jackson to confirm it." Nash led Sidney over to a bale of straw.

"Well? Did he?" Sidney asked, climbing onto Nash's lap.

"Yeah," he mumbled.

Sidney could tell there had been more to the conversation between Nash and Jackson. The relationship between Sidney and his dad had always been strained, but since Jackson had started a new family, their relationship was non-existent. "What else?"

It took Nash several moments to speak. "Jackson bought Diablo for stud purposes, but he soon figured out it wouldn't be possible for Diablo to breed the old fashioned way. Instead of investing money to collect Diablo's sperm and freezing it, he thought whipping the horse every time he tried to mount one of the geldings would be easier."

Shocked at his dad's cruelty, Sidney couldn't help but

think Jackson's reaction to Diablo's preferences went beyond the stallion. He thought of all the times his dad had hit him over the years. Did those blows have more to do with who he was than what he'd done?

Sidney climbed off Nash's lap before walking to the open door once more. He picked up the binoculars and watched the two horses until his vision clouded with tears. Diablo seemed happy for the first time in nearly three years. "I wonder if we'll ever get him back in his stall."

Strong arms wrapped around him from behind. "I don't know that we need to, at least not until the weather changes. The bigger question is how Diablo will react to people while in the pasture with Buckwheat?"

Sidney leant back against Nash. "We'll have to go slow."

"Yep," Nash agreed.

After setting the binoculars aside, Sidney turned around and pressed his cheek against Nash's chest. "I don't ever want to see my dad again." It was a hard thing to face, but Sidney knew in his heart the man would never accept him, and Sidney was tired of trying.

Nash ran comforting hands up and down Sidney's back. "I think more time apart wouldn't be a bad thing, but never say never." He rubbed his lips across Sidney's forehead. "Let's go fix us some dinner. I got a new movie I want you to watch."

Sidney smiled. Since being introduced to Sidney's brand of entertainment, Nash had become quite the collector. He was presently obsessed with policemen for some reason. "More cops?"

"Nope. Mechanics."

Sidney's interest was piqued. "Muscled mechanics?"

"Yep. Sweaty, greasy, muscled mechanics with big dicks."

"Oh, fuck. That's like the perfect storm of porn." Sidney's cock went rigid in his jeans. "How about we grab a couple beers and some bread 'n peanut butter on the way through the kitchen?"

"Forget the bread and you've got yourself a deal."

Chapter Ten

June 1989

As much as Sidney hated spending his summers in school, the added classes had put him ahead of schedule. Nine more months, he told himself. Although the closer he came to graduation, the more he worried. His grades were top notch, so he shouldn't have a problem getting a job in either Kansas City or Wichita, but was that really where he wanted to be?

Noise from downstairs drew his attention. "Is that you?" he called.

"Yep. Where're you at?" Nash asked.

"Studio." Sidney glanced around the old master bedroom. He never had been able to bring himself to sleep in the same room where his mom had died, but he found the light was perfect for a workroom.

Sidney set his pencil down on the drafting table before spinning his chair to face the door. He'd purposely not visited the barn upon his arrival home from college. The news that Buckwheat had come down with colic had devastated everyone who worked the ranch. Although they'd caught Buckwheat's condition early, according to Nash, the horse wasn't responding to treatment.

He braced himself for the news he knew in his heart would come. The door opened and the man he loved came into the room. Nash looked like shit, and Sidney suddenly felt guilty for not seeking him out earlier. "How is he?"

With his hands in his pockets, Nash looked down at the floor, shielding his face from Sidney's view with his hat.

"Not good." Nash shook his head with a sigh. "Doc thinks it's time we put him out of his misery."

Sidney jumped to his feet. "We can't do that. What about Diablo?"

Nash looked up with tears in his eyes. "Nothing's working, and Doc doesn't think Buckwheat'll live through surgery."

Sidney swallowed around the lump in his throat. "Can we try anyway?"

Nash crossed the room before wrapping Sidney in his arms. "Come down to the barn. I think it'll help you understand what I'm talking about."

Sidney buried his face against Nash's chest. Whether it was being in her room or the hopelessness of the situation, Sidney didn't know, but all he could think about were the hours leading up to his mom's death. His dad had tried to keep him out of the room, but Sidney would sit on the floor outside the door listening to the most important person in his world struggle to breathe.

Although he didn't know everything there was to know about horses, Sidney knew what colic did to them. "I can't."

"Then let me do what needs to be done." Nash kissed the top of Sidney's head. "I'm so sorry."

"Not your fault," Sidney said, struggling with his emotions. "Doc already confirmed it had nothing to do with parasites. It's just one of those things that happen." But why did it have to happen to Buckwheat, why not Rosie or one of the other horses? Sidney squeezed his eyes shut but eventually nodded his consent. "Would you call me from the barn once it's done? I'd like to say goodbye."

"Yeah." Nash tilted Sidney's chin up for a soft kiss. "We'll go ahead and load him onto the trailer before..." Nash stopped long enough to clear his throat. The emotional situation was obviously getting to him. "I'll put some straw down. Make sure he's as comfortable as possible."

Sidney's gaze strayed to where his mom's bed had once sat. Would his mom have wanted to be euthanized if given the option? Although he'd been so young at the time, Sidney knew she'd held on as long as she could for his sake. Wouldn't it have been better had she been able to slip into a never-ending sleep instead of gasping until her lungs completely gave out?

"Where's Diablo?" he asked.

"In his stall, sedated. We tried to leave him in the pasture, but he busted through the fence. He'll have a few new scars, but nothing serious."

Sidney thought of Nash and how the cowboy had sat quietly with him on the day of his mom's funeral. He pulled away from Nash and squared his shoulders. "I'll go keep Diablo company while you take care of Buckwheat."

"You don't have to. Sedated or not, I doubt he'd let you near him at this point."

"Doesn't matter. I'll sit across the barn if I have to. The important thing is that he sees he's not completely alone."

* * * *

Carrying a small cooler and a bag of burgers, Nash entered the barn. Sidney was still keeping vigil at Diablo's stall, staring off into space. It had been hours since they'd driven Buckwheat's body to the crematorium behind the vet's office.

"Hey," Nash greeted, bending to give Sidney a quick kiss. "Thought you might be hungry." He set the cooler on the ground beside Sidney before pulling a bale of straw over to sit on. "How's he doing?"

Sidney shrugged. "That extra shot Doc gave him hasn't worn off yet, but I'm afraid of what'll happen when it does."

Nash dug into the sack and withdrew a cheeseburger. "Here."

Sidney shook his head. "No thanks."

Nash's instinct was to argue with the younger man and demand he eat something, but in the end, he put the burger back into the bag and set it on top of the cooler.

"I've been thinking about my dad," Sidney said after a few moments.

"Really?" Sidney hadn't mentioned Jackson in over a year.

"Yeah. He stayed with her up to the end. He watched the woman he loved die in his arms." Sidney looked over at Nash. "He was never the same after that. Not that he was a prince before, but..."

Nash held out his arms. "Come here, babe."

Sidney immediately took Nash up on the offer and climbed into his lap. Nash tried to wrap a protective cocoon around the man he loved.

"Promise me something," Sidney whispered.

"Anything," Nash agreed.

"If anything happens to me, promise you won't let it change you like my dad and Josh did."

Nash buried his face in Sidney's long hair. Sidney hadn't mentioned Luke or Josh since going to the rehabilitation hospital almost two years earlier. Luke had asked to see him, but Josh had still refused to talk to Sidney. Although Luke's condition was permanent, he'd worked hard to regain the use of his voice. According to Sidney, it had been a very emotional visit, but one he didn't ever care to talk about.

"I can't promise that," Nash finally answered.

Sidney sat back enough to stare into Nash's eyes. He opened his mouth as if to argue, but closed it with a sigh. "I guess I couldn't promise you either," he said after a few minutes.

Nash continued to hold Sidney until the interior of the barn became so dark he could no longer see Diablo. "Want me to go in and grab the sleeping bags?"

"Yeah."

Nash stood before depositing Sidney back on his chair. "I won't be long."

* * * *

135

A noise that sounded like the barn was falling down around him woke Sidney. "Diablo!" he yelled at the stallion's cry.

Nash was on his feet before Sidney could get himself untangled from the sleeping bag. "Turn on the light," Nash ordered as another crash sounded.

Naked, Sidney rushed to the control box beside the front door and lifted the lever. The lights came on, illuminating the barn in a golden glow. He rushed back to the stall, heedless of his nudity, to find Nash trying to get a rope around Diablo's neck.

Blood splattered Nash's face and hands as Diablo continued to kick the back wall of the barn. Sidney stepped up beside Nash to try to help.

"Get back!" Nash yelled.

"Tell me what to do?" Sidney asked. The sight of the ragged cut on Diablo's neck didn't bode well for the stallion.

When a loud squeal sounded from Diablo seconds before he dropped to the ground, Sidney's heart sank. "I'll call Doc."

"No." Nash dropped the rope along with his head.

"Nash?"

"He'll be dead before Doc can get here," Nash mumbled, rubbing his eyes with the heels of his hands.

Diablo continued to squeal in pain as he thumped his head against the floor.

Nash looked over his shoulder at Sidney. "Get me the gun."

Sidney backed up, shaking his head.

"Dammit, Sidney, I don't want to do it, but I've got no fucking choice!" Nash yelled, choking on his last word. "He's going to lie here and beat his own fucking head in if I don't do something. Now go!"

Sidney turned and ran. The darkness of the ranch yard combined with his free-flowing tears prevented him from seeing the boot scraper just outside the barn. Before he could right himself, Sidney went down hard on the gravel drive, the stones cutting into his hands and chin.

Rolling to his back, Sidney shook his stinging hands and tried to regain his breath. Fuck. He struggled to his feet, giving himself a moment to get his balance before taking off towards the house once more.

He pushed a chair to the kitchen door, cursing his height once again. Sidney lifted the loaded rifle off its rack and jumped to the floor, paying attention to holding the rifle away from him.

By the time he made it back to the barn, Diablo's screams were unbearable. It was obvious the horse's pain was more than physical. Sidney handed the rifle to Nash.

Nash did a double take when he reached for the rifle. "What happened?"

Sidney waved his bloody hand. "Just do it."

"Not until you leave," Nash said.

Would Nash forever try to shelter Sidney from the pain of real life? He turned his back and crossed his arms. "Just do it, please."

Sidney held his breath, waiting for the shot he knew would come. His body jerked as the rifle fired.

An anguished cry escaped Nash moments later.

Sidney turned around to find Nash on his knees, the rifle on the scarred wooden floor beside him. Without looking into the stall, Sidney went to Nash. Wrapping his arms around the man he loved, he knew it was a day that would haunt both of them for the rest of their lives.

* * * *

After making the call to Doc, Sidney ran upstairs to his bathroom and dug out the first aid kit. The skinned spots on his hands and chin weren't serious, but they needed to be cleaned and disinfected. He started with an antibacterial soap, wincing as he scrubbed the abraded areas. Sidney's gaze went back to the white metal box that his mom had first filled with supplies. Although he should probably use the alcohol, he grabbed the peroxide instead.

Sidney smiled as he poured the clear, odourless liquid onto the palm of his left hand. He remembered how fascinated he'd been as a kid when his mom would pour the peroxide on and the white bubbles would foam up around whatever wound he'd happened to get that day.

He cupped his hand and poured a good amount into his palm before bringing his chin down to dip into the tiny pool of antiseptic. Sidney stared at his reflection in the mirror as the bubbles did their job.

Satisfied gangrene wouldn't set in anytime soon, Sidney pulled on a pair of shorts before heading back downstairs. He decided to make a pot of coffee since he doubted either of them would be able to sleep. Diablo would need to be removed, but they wouldn't be able to accomplish that until the ranch hands arrived for work.

Coffee on, Sidney stared out of the window above the kitchen sink. Although he knew Diablo's death would haunt him for years to come, it was Nash Sidney worried about. The torment in Nash's expression when he'd handed the rifle to Sidney and ordered him back to the house to call Doc would forever be etched in his memory. He'd known without asking that Nash planned to stay in the barn and clean up the blood before the ranch hands made it to work. Never in Sidney's life had he seen so much blood.

The car accident flashed through his mind, only it had been Sidney's blood covering the inside of the car on that stretch of New Jersey road. Luke's injuries had been more internal. For the first time since the accident, a memory of Josh pulled from the depths of Sidney's mind.

He remembered lying on the front seat, the buck still half in, half out of the car. Josh was screaming at a passing car for help. Sidney had tried to talk, to tell Josh his brother had gone through the windshield, but the words wouldn't come.

Josh's face as he tore off his shirt and pressed it to Sidney's cheek was eerily like Nash's expression in the barn. It was the first time Sidney remembered Josh apologising. Over and over Josh told Sidney how sorry he was. Why would Josh be apologising to him?

Once Sidney was able to tell Josh to go and help Luke, Josh's eyes had rounded. Josh had jerked back and covered his mouth with his hand. Sidney hadn't understood the reaction, he still didn't.

Sidney rubbed his chest. The tightening that came with the memories of that night was worse this time. It had been a while since he'd tried to reach out to Josh. Maybe he should try again before too much time passed.

With new resolve to mend an old friendship that meant the world to him, Sidney filled an old Thermos with coffee before heading out to the barn.

Stepping inside the barn, Sidney didn't immediately see Nash, but he heard a noise coming from Diablo's stall. "I brought coffee," he said, crossing the expanse.

"I thought I told you to stay in the house," Nash's gruff-sounding voice called.

Sidney continued on. When he saw Nash he nearly dropped the Thermos to the floor. He caught it in time and set it down, his heart racing. "I thought you might need me," he said, stepping over the largest pool of blood to kneel at Nash's side.

Nash continued to stare at the gaping hole in Diablo's head. "What I need is for you not to be touched by this. Go back inside."

"No," Sidney whispered, putting his palm in the centre of Nash's back.

That was all it took to finally get Nash's attention. Nash blinked several times before turning to address Sidney. The confused expression on Nash's face said it all. "What?"

"I'm not ten anymore, Nash. You can't just fix everything for me." Sidney gestured to the dead stallion. "This? This is real life. It's ugly and messy, but it needs to be dealt with, and I want to help."

Nash's eyes filled with tears. "Okay." He took a deep

breath before brushing a kiss across Sidney's lips. "I'll go to the equipment shed and get the bag of oil absorbent. You start clearing away the sawdust."

When Nash started to get to his feet, Sidney held onto his hand and pulled him back down. There was something in Nash's voice that worried him, and Sidney couldn't let the moment pass without reassuring himself. "Are you okay?"

Nash broke eye contact and glanced at Diablo once again. "I will be." Nash kissed Sidney again, more deeply and with more emotion.

* * * *

September 1989

Sitting in his rented studio apartment, Sidney dug out the small slip of paper from his wallet with Josh's phone number scribbled on it. He'd had to practically threaten Josh to get it, but he'd eventually relented. Sidney figured it was Josh's way of getting Sidney to go away.

He dialled the number and waited, hoping like hell Josh would pick up.

"Hello?"

Sidney heard noises in the background, and Josh seemed out of breath. Not the best way to start off a conversation. "Hey," he finally said. "It's Sidney."

"Hey," Josh returned. "Listen, this isn't a good time. Can I call you back later?"

At any other time, Sidney might believe Josh was just trying to put him off, but the commotion in the background told Sidney otherwise. "Sure. Do you still have my numbers?"

"Yeah, I'm sure they're around here somewhere," Josh replied. A loud crash sounded. "Shit. Gotta go."

The phone went dead before Sidney could say anything more. He wondered what life must be like for Josh and Luke. Although Luke had made remarkable strides since the accident, Sidney knew from talking to Maggie that

Luke still required almost constant supervision. Despite her misgivings on the matter, Josh had insisted he be the one to care for his brother. Not only had Josh dropped out of school, but according to Maggie, he'd dropped out of life, too, centring his attention on Luke.

Sidney was once again thankful he'd convinced Maggie to sue Sidney's insurance company for damages. Of course Sidney had been dropped by the insurance company, but at least he slept a little better at night knowing the Ballentines had enough money to care for their son.

Feeling down, he called the one person who always had the ability to cheer him up. Although Nash had been distant the last few times Sidney had been home, he was still there, something Sidney couldn't say about anyone else in his life.

"Running E."

"Lonnie?" Sidney asked, wondering why the ranch hand was answering the phone instead of Nash.

"Yep. Nash is in Hutchinson again so he asked me to answer the barn phone if it rang."

Hutch? It was the third time in two weeks that he'd called only to find out Nash was out. "Did he say when he'd be back?" Jealousy began to creep its way up Sidney's spine. There was only one reason he could think of that would make Nash drive into Hutch three times in two weeks. *Reece.*

"Nope, but usually we're gone by the time he gets back," Lonnie said.

"Okay, thanks." Sidney hung up the phone. It was only Thursday, which meant he had another entire day of classes before he could head back to the ranch. He glanced at the finished assignment. It was due in the morning, but perhaps Professor Garmin would let him hand it in early?

The whole idea behind the project pissed him off anyway. Sidney hadn't decided whether or not to believe the professor when he said it was a contest to see who could come up with the best design for a new library being built just north of Chicago.

In Sidney's opinion, the company that had set up the contest was just looking for a free design, but because Garmin was going to give them a grade, Sidney had little choice in the matter.

He pulled out his planner, intending to call his professor. His next move would be to try and find an address for Reece Lyons.

Chapter Eleven

By the time Grady Nash pulled his truck into the drive it was almost eleven thirty, and he still had a few hours' worth of work to do before he could go to bed. He started towards the barn, but slowed when he spotted Sidney's big Bronco parked next to the house. "What the hell?"

Nash parked beside the Bronco and got out. He was surprised to see Sidney sitting on the darkened porch smoking a cigarette, a habit Nash thought the younger man had given up years earlier. "What's going on?"

Sidney blew out a puff of smoke. "I was about to ask you the same thing."

Something in Sidney's tone stopped Nash in his tracks. "Well, as you can tell, I'm just getting home. I had something to do. The question is, what're you doing home on a Thursday?"

Sidney flicked the cigarette onto the brown grass beside the porch. "I called earlier. Lonnie told me you went to Hutch again." Sidney stood and put his hands on his lean hips. "You've been going there quite a bit lately."

"Yeah." The more Sidney talked, the madder Nash became.

"Only one reason I could think of that you'd be visiting Hutch so often, so I drove by Reece's house but your truck wasn't there."

Nash took a step back. The accusation cut to the bone, and if he wasn't careful, he'd lash out just as deeply. He turned on his heels and walked back down the porch steps. "Go back to school, Sidney," he said over his shoulder as he stalked towards the barn.

"Oh no you don't," Sidney called. In moments, Sidney had jumped in front of Nash, trying to stop him.

Nash wasn't having it. He stepped around Sidney and continued on, his hands fisted at his sides. He'd been in a bad mood to begin with. The last thing he had the energy for was a hissy fit from a jealous lover.

Nash made it to the barn before his anger exploded. He turned around and backed Sidney against the barn door. "Have I ever. Ever! Given you cause to doubt my love for you?"

Without giving Sidney a chance to answer, Nash continued. "I haven't seen Reece in almost five fucking years!"

"Then what're you doing in Hutch all the time? Huh?" Sidney asked, not backing down.

"Gettin' my goddamn GED, okay?" Nash huffed out a breath and turned to walk towards Diablo's stall. Over the last couple of weeks, he'd spent a good amount of thinking time staring into the empty space.

Sidney moved up next to him to lean on the worn wood. "What're you talking about? I thought you graduated."

Nash shook his head. It was one of the few things in his life he'd wished he could do over again. "No. My dad was killed my senior year. I kinda went off track for a few months and flunked a couple of my required classes. The school felt bad for me, so they let me walk across the stage at graduation and receive an unsigned diploma. I was supposed to take summer school to make up my grades, but I started working here instead."

Nash concentrated on the dark stain still visible on the old wood floor. "I've been taking some refresher courses so I could finally become a high school graduate."

Sidney wrapped his arms around Nash's waist, but it didn't help Nash's mood. He glanced down and stared into Sidney's big green eyes. "Do you have any idea how much it hurts to know you'd think I'd cheat on you? Fuck! I've devoted my entire adult life to you."

144

Nash pulled away from Sidney's embrace. "Go on into the house. I just need some time to cool down."

"I'm so sorry I doubted you," Sidney said, trying once again to hold Nash.

Nash stepped away. "Please, Sidney, just give me a few minutes."

Although it was obvious Sidney didn't want to go anywhere, he eventually sighed and left the barn. Nash opened the gate on Diablo's stall and went inside. He sat on the bare floor with his back against the wall and promptly fell apart.

It wasn't the accusation that continued to cling to him; it was the first real peek at the fragility of his relationship. What if he went through with his plan to change his entire future only to see the relationship end somewhere down the line?

Nash took off his hat before resting his head against the short wall separating Diablo's stall from the next. He'd tried to push the memories of the night the stallion had died behind him, but they just wouldn't leave. It was affecting his job. Rarely did he want anything to do with the cattle or the few horses remaining. Nash knew the truth. He was already withdrawing, saying goodbye to his old life. He'd seen the truth of his situation the night he'd been forced to put a bullet through Diablo's brain.

Nash got to his feet and resettled the hat on his head. He could only imagine what Sidney was doing at that moment. No doubt the man was pacing back and forth on the porch, puffing away on one of those fucking cigarettes. That was another thing the two of them needed to get settled between them, and by God, Nash didn't plan to let the sun come up without some kind of resolution to their problems.

* * * *

Sidney was staring at the contents of the refrigerator when Nash came in. He didn't bother looking up—he'd seen enough disgust on Nash's face for one day. "Hungry?"

"Yeah." Nash hauled Sidney backwards and shut the fridge. "But not for food, at least not yet."

Sidney was confused by Nash's actions. It had only been about fifteen minutes since Nash had ordered Sidney out of the barn. He let Nash lead him by the hand towards the living room. The last thing Sidney wanted was to get yelled at again. Sure he'd been an asshole for accusing Nash of cheating, but what did Nash expect when he kept important details from him? He still couldn't wrap his mind around the fact that Nash thought he had to hide his actions.

Nash sat on the couch before pulling Sidney down onto his lap. "I want to sell the stock."

Shocked, Sidney's jaw dropped. Was Nash trying to cut all ties with Sidney over one stupid fight? "What? Why?"

Nash shrugged. "Because the time's come for me to make a decision, and I've made it."

Sidney's gut clenched. "What kind of decision?"

"For the last five years, you've been trying to live in two worlds in order to be with me. It's worked out okay with you being in school, but it'll be a different thing entirely once you graduate in a couple of months."

Was Nash saying what Sidney thought he was saying? "So you're just giving up the ranch to run off to some unknown city with me?"

Nash settled his hands on Sidney's hips before pulling him closer. The action put Sidney's ass right over Nash's half-hard cock. "I still don't know how the hell I'm going to make a living in the city, but I can't stay here without you."

Sidney rested his head on Nash's shoulder. He wondered... "Does this have something to do with Diablo's death?"

"It has everything to do with it." Nash moved to grip Sidney's arms. He pushed him upright enough to stare into Sidney's eyes. "Do you know how I was able to pull that trigger?"

Sidney wasn't sure what to say. "Because you're stronger than I am?" No way could Sidney have ended Diablo's life.

"Nope. Because when I looked into that horses eyes and saw not only the physical pain he was in but the emotional pain as well, I knew I had no other choice. If I lost you, I'd most likely put a bullet in my own brain. Because without you, I'm just an empty shell. You're the one who makes my heart beat. I saw the same thing in Diablo's eyes that night, and with no hope of bringing his love back, I did what he was trying to do for himself."

The admission stunned Sidney. He knew the stallion's death had plagued Nash, but evidently not for the reason Sidney had thought. "What happens if you give up everything and figure out I'm not worth it?"

"I won't." Nash brushed Sidney's hair behind his shoulders before pulling him in for a passionate kiss.

Sidney accepted everything Nash offered, the kiss, and the man's desire to follow him to the city. He would have taken the time to question Nash further regarding his plans, but Sidney could tell by the emotional kiss Nash had had enough for one night.

Pulling back, Sidney broke their kiss. "Let's go upstairs."

Before Sidney knew what was happening, he was thrown over Nash's shoulder like a one hundred and thirty pound bag of potatoes. Sidney squealed and reached down to slap Nash's tight jean-clad ass. "I'll get you back for this."

"Promise?" Nash chuckled, taking the steps two at a time.

Tossed onto the bed, Sidney bounced several times before settling on the mattress. He stopped laughing when he noticed the serious expression back on Nash's handsome face. "What?"

Instead of taking the time to unbutton his shirt, Nash pulled it off over his head. He remained silent until he was fully undressed. Crawling onto the bed, Nash began to remove Sidney's clothing piece by piece. "I want to be the one you come home to every night."

An image of the two of them growing old together came to mind. "I want that, too."

Some of Nash's worry seemed to lift from his shoulders.

He peeled Sidney's jeans and underwear off in one smooth move. Nash lay on his back and pulled Sidney on top of him. "Even though I don't like the reason you came home early, I'm glad you're here."

Sidney wanted to forget his jealousy, but Nash deserved another apology. "I'm sorry I doubted you. I guess I still have a hard time believing I'm enough."

One moment Sidney was on top and the next Nash rolled over, putting Sidney under him. "Enough?" Nash ground his hard cock against Sidney. "You're every dream I ever had come to life. You're my family, my lover and my best friend. How could I possibly ask for more?"

Sidney smiled up at his big, handsome cowboy. "Good answer." He wrapped his legs around Nash, enjoying the feel of Nash's pubic hair as it rubbed against his cock. Opening his mouth, he welcomed Nash's kiss. Kissing had always been a major aphrodisiac for Sidney and it only seemed to get stronger the longer he was with Nash.

He whimpered into the kiss, needing to feel the stretch of Nash's length slide inside him. Blindly, Sidney reached towards the drawer but fell short of his goal. He broke the kiss and smiled up at Nash. "Would you mind using those long arms of yours to get the lube?"

Nash surprised a chuckle out of Sidney when he quickly flicked his tongue in and out of his mouth. "How about some natural lube?"

It was rare that Nash acted silly. Sidney didn't know if it had something to do with his dad dying or if he'd always been serious, but the goofy grin was enough to send Sidney into a fit of the giggles. Although he enjoyed the hard, fast fucks they indulged in most of the time, the events earlier left him yearning for more. "Make love to me," he whispered once the giggles subsided.

Nash's expression turned serious. "I've done nothing but that since the first night we were together."

Sidney tightened his legs that wrapped around Nash as he reached up and cupped the sweet man's face with both hands. "That's probably the nicest thing anyone's ever said to me."

"I meant it." Nash turned his head and kissed Sidney's palm. "I love you."

A soul-deep smile blossomed from within Sidney. "I know. I could say I knew since the time you saved my ass when you painted Dad's porch after I wrecked it, but that would just be creepy."

Nash chuckled. He reached over and grabbed the lube from the bedside table. "So when did you know?"

Sidney thought back over everything Nash had done for him. "You told me I was sexy even when I was cut up with no hair."

"You were." Nash rimmed Sidney's hole with his slicked fingers.

"I wouldn't have been to anyone who didn't love me. That's when I knew." Sidney felt his eyes sting at the admission. He quickly blinked away the moisture. "By the way, I fell in love with you the day you carried the can of paint to the porch."

Nash eased two fingers into Sidney's channel as he leant down for a kiss. It didn't take long before Sidney's body needed more. He reached between them and slapped at Nash's hand, having no desire to break their kiss.

Nash withdrew his tongue and chuckled again. "Okay, I get the hint." He removed his fingers before replacing them with his cock.

Sidney took a deep breath before exhaling as Nash's length worked its way inside him. With one hand on his own chest, Sidney squeezed one of his sensitive nipples before reaching with his free hand to torture Nash's chest.

Nash let out a grunt and bucked his hips when Sidney pinched the tender flesh. "You know that drives me crazy."

"Yeah." Sidney did it again, applying even more force. Each time he tweaked his own nipple, he felt it in his cock.

Nash growled and repositioned Sidney's legs over his shoulders. He began moving in and out of Sidney's body in quick, short thrusts. Just when Sidney was becoming accustomed to the rhythm, Nash changed it.

The deep, hard slam of Nash's body against Sidney's hole drew a squeak out of Sidney. Where the hell had that come from?

Nash laughed and shook his head before pounding deep once again.

"Fuck!" Sidney cried when his teeth rattled. "You can only go so deep, love."

"Really? Let's make sure." Nash practically folded Sidney in two before starting again.

With each plunge of Nash's cock, Sidney grew closer to climax. His pre cum began to drip from the head of his cock onto his chest. It was one of the most erotic things he'd ever experienced. "More," he begged.

Nash obliged with a grunt and thrust of his hips, grinding himself against Sidney's ass after pushing in deep.

Sidney cried Nash's name as the first strand of cum shot from his cock. The warm seed landed on his chin. Sidney quickly tilted his head down and opened his mouth, hoping to catch a taste of himself on his tongue.

Although Sidney was only able to capture a few drops, they were enough to set Nash off.

"Don't swallow," Nash ordered, his face screwing up with the intensity of his orgasm.

Sidney held the slightly bitter cum on his outstretched tongue while Nash rode out his climax. He removed his legs from Nash's shoulders and pulled the man he loved down on top of him.

Nash's tongue swiped across Sidney's, capturing Sidney's essence, before delving inside for a deep kiss.

Sidney moaned into the kiss as Nash's softened cock fell out of his body. His stomach growled, reminding Sidney he hadn't eaten in hours, but he was too comfortable to move. He smiled despite the tongue probing the inside of his mouth. There would be time for food tomorrow. Tonight was too special. He finally allowed himself to dream of a real future with Nash that went beyond college.

* * * *

The phone rang while Sidney was putting a tuna casserole in the oven. He shut the door and made sure the temperature was correct before crossing the kitchen to the phone. "Hello?"

"Sidney?"

Sidney's heart skipped a beat at the familiar voice. "Yeah. How're you doing, Josh?"

"I'm okay, I guess. Luke fell trying to get to the couch yesterday. I guess I just didn't want you to think I was making an excuse not to talk when you called."

"Did he hurt himself?" Sidney squeezed his eyes shut. He wanted to reach out to the brothers but was afraid of being shot down by Josh.

"Bruised, but otherwise the same." Josh cleared his voice. "I told him you'd called, and he wanted to make sure I called you back." Josh made a sound in his throat Sidney couldn't identify. "Hell, I would've called you back anyway. I've been doing a lot of thinking about shit."

Sidney wanted to say something but kept his mouth shut. It was the first time since the accident Josh had sought Sidney out.

"I miss you. I know you may never want to see me again after the way I treated you when you came up before, but…"

"I do," Sidney said, cutting his friend off. "I think about you every day."

Josh sighed. "So…I was talking to my mom the other day, and she thought it would be nice if you came up for Thanksgiving like you used to."

Sidney winced. He'd love to reconnect with the Ballentine family again. "I'll talk to Nash about it, but we usually go down to Phoenix to see his mom on Thanksgiving."

"Oh. That's okay. I'm sure Mom will understand."

"No, don't tell her anything until I speak to Nash. His mom's been seeing someone anyway, so maybe she'd rather spend the holiday with him and his family. Nash should be in anytime for dinner, so I can talk to him then. He is invited, right?"

"Sure. We all know he's part of your life now."

Sidney wondered how Luke would react to Nash. The two of them had never met, and Sidney would be lying if he said a meeting wouldn't make him nervous. "Okay. I'll give you a call later this evening."

"Thanks."

Sidney hung up the phone with a lighter heart. He knew he'd do everything in his power to travel east instead of west for Thanksgiving. He'd waited too long for the invitation to pass it up.

* * * *

November 1989

Nash knocked on the bathroom door. "You almost ready?"

"Yeah. Just a sec," Sidney answered.

Nash crossed the room to the wall of windows. The view of Philadelphia was breathtaking, but Nash still felt like one of a million ants the moment he stepped foot out of the hotel.

Despite his resolve to move wherever Sidney's career called him, he was beginning to worry. It was one thing to think you were ready for such a drastic lifestyle change, but it was completely different to actually make the leap from country boy to city dweller.

The bathroom door opened moments before Sidney's arms wrapped around Nash's waist. It was a good reminder of why he'd made the decision in the first place. Even in a place as foreign to him as Philadelphia, one touch from Sidney and Nash began to relax.

"I love this city," Sidney said.

"It's pretty, that's for sure," Nash agreed. He turned and gave Sidney a brief kiss, slipping his love only a little tongue before pulling back. The dark green dress shirt set off Sidney's colouring perfectly. "You look good."

"Thanks." Sidney bit his bottom lip. "I'll never be able to thank you enough for coming here with me. I know you're mom wasn't very happy."

"Don't worry about her. She was fine once I told her we'd come for a week after you're finished with school." Nash didn't say more. For whatever reason, his mom just hadn't warmed to Sidney like Nash had hoped she would. She wasn't mean or anything, but Nash could tell she'd rather have him all to herself on Thanksgiving. The first time he'd informed her Sidney was coming down with him, his mom had pitched a fit, but Nash had made it clear he wouldn't come if Sidney wasn't invited. So they continued to make the yearly trip even though all three of them were on edge the entire time.

"We'd better go." Sidney pulled away and picked up his winter coat.

"Sounds good. I called down for the car earlier so it should be waiting for us." Nash grabbed his coat before leaving the room.

Despite Josh's offer to pick them up from the airport, Nash had preferred to rent a car. Of course he hadn't counted on the amount of traffic he'd have to drive in. "You wanna drive since you know the way?"

"Sure." Sidney gave the valet some money before getting behind the wheel.

Nash buckled his seat belt. His stomach was in knots, but he tried not to let it show. Sidney needed this reunion to work, and Nash would do everything in his power to make sure it did.

* * * *

Pulling into the circular driveway, Sidney was surprised

to see so many cars. It wasn't until he remembered how long it had been since he'd seen the family that he realised the extra cars probably belonged to the Ballentine brothers.

Nash whistled as the car came to a stop. "Pretty fancy."

"Yeah," Sidney agreed. "You wouldn't know they had money if you didn't see stuff like that though." Sidney gestured to the row of expensive European cars. One older van stood out from the rest. Sidney could tell it was wheelchair accessible. His stomach sank. It was a very real reminder of Luke's paralysis. Although Luke had regained some use of his hands, he would forever be confined to a wheelchair.

Sidney got out of the car before he changed his mind and drove them back to the airport. "You can do this," he whispered to himself.

"Okay?" Nash asked, joining Sidney on the sidewalk leading to the front steps.

Sidney grabbed Nash's hand. "Just nervous."

"You and me both." Nash led Sidney up the steps to the door. "Ready?" he asked, his finger poised over the doorbell.

After a deep, hopefully calming, breath, Sidney nodded. "Do it."

* * * *

Although the afternoon had been fantastic, Sidney couldn't help but feel Josh was avoiding him. He'd tried several times to get Josh alone, but his friend managed to come up with several excuses why he couldn't at the moment.

With Nash heavily involved in watching the football game with the rest of the Ballentine men, Sidney retreated to the kitchen. Maybe helping Maggie with the dishes would make the time go faster. "Can I help?"

Elbows-deep in sudsy water, Maggie smiled. "You sure can. Grab a towel out of the drawer."

Sidney did as instructed before taking up position next to Maggie. "Dishwasher on the fritz?"

"No." She held up a plate. "These belonged to Alan's mother. They came to me with strict instructions to never put them in the dishwasher." Maggie grinned. "Before we got them, we just used regular plates. I'm not sure, but I think my mother-in-law just wanted to torture me on holidays."

Sidney chuckled. "You should've had girls instead of boys."

"Or boys who were interested in getting married and providing me with daughters-in-law," Maggie fired back.

They continued to wash and dry dishes with idle conversation. Sidney held out as long as he could before finally laying his cards on the table. "Does Josh blame me?"

Scrubbing the gravy boat, Maggie suddenly looked thoughtful. "No. Josh seems to carry a lot of guilt about the accident. He hates himself for making you drive at all, especially after you told him you didn't want to. Do you know he hasn't tasted a drop of liquor since? That's another thing that bothers him. He knows if he hadn't been drunk, Luke would've been safe in the back seat."

"None of it was Josh's fault," Sidney argued.

"What happened, happened. It wasn't anyone's fault. Funny how Luke seems to be the only one who understands that." Maggie gave Sidney a reassuring smile. "If I know my son, Josh is probably out behind the garage smoking."

Sidney couldn't help but chuckle. "You know?"

Maggie rolled her eyes. "I've always known what my boys do when they think I'm not watching." She pointed towards the coat hanging beside the door. "Take Alan's."

"Thanks." Sidney grabbed the coat before heading outside. He jogged to the detached garage behind the house. "Josh?" he called, trying to give the man some warning.

"Back here."

Sidney rounded the corner. "Your mom told me you'd be out here smoking."

"Fuck." Josh shook his head. "She's been after me to quit. I thought her nagging was bad until Luke decided to start in on me, too." He held out the pack. "Want one?"

It had been weeks since Sidney had smoked. He licked his lips and looked around before accepting. "Thanks."

Josh chuckled before taking another deep drag. "Nash after you to quit?"

"Yeah." Sidney inhaled and closed his eyes. *Ahhh, fuck* he missed it. "God, this is good."

Josh's hand landed on Sidney's shoulder. He didn't say anything for the longest time. The two of them just stood there, smoking and looking out at the trees at the back of the property. "I'm glad you're okay," Josh finally said.

Sidney looked up at his friend. "It wasn't your fault, ya know?"

Josh removed his hand and shrugged. "Whatever."

"No. I won't stand by and let you carry this bullshit on your own." Sidney moved to stand in front of Josh. Even if Josh hated him for the rest of his life, Sidney needed his friend to know the truth. "You were passed out in the backseat and Luke unfastened his seatbelt and kissed me. I saw the deer dart out into the road, but I couldn't push Luke into the seat fast enough before we hit it."

"I know," Josh mumbled. "Luke told me a long time ago."

"So why're you still blaming yourself?"

Josh broke eye contact and stared over Sidney's shoulder. "Because I need to blame someone and I love you and Luke too much for that."

"What?" Sidney stumbled backwards. "How can you say something like that? For the last five years you've wanted nothing to do with me."

Josh shook his head adamantly. "No. I didn't want anything to do with myself! To this day, every time I look at you, I see them."

Sidney's hand rose to his cheek. With Nash's help, Sidney had become so used to his scars he often forgot the outside world still noticed them.

Josh captured Sidney's hand. "You were so beautiful," he mumbled, tears filling his eyes.

Squaring his shoulders, Sidney stared up at Josh. "I still am. Just ask Nash." At that moment, Sidney wanted the comfort only Nash could provide. He pulled his hand from Josh's grip. "I'm sorry you can't see beyond them."

Sidney started towards the house but stopped before he rounded the corner of the garage and looked back at Josh. "Luke may be in a wheelchair, and I may not look the same, but you're the one who lost your life in that accident."

"I know! That's what I've been trying to tell you!" Josh screamed as Sidney made it to the back door.

* * * *

Nash was packing their clothes when there was a knock on the door. He glanced at the closed bathroom door, hoping the sound hadn't disturbed Sidney. On his way to the door, Nash grabbed the keycard. He had a good idea who their visitor was, and he'd be damned if he'd let Josh into the room.

He stepped out into the hall before quietly pulling the door shut behind him. "What do you want, Josh?"

With his hands in his front jeans pockets, Josh shuffled from foot to foot. "I need to talk to Sidney."

"No, you don't. What you need is to let go of whatever you're drowning in and get some help." Nash narrowed his eyes. "Before you pull two good men down with you."

"I know." Josh took his hands out of his pockets before rubbing his eyes. "That's what I came to tell him. I talked it over with my family and they've agreed to help take care of Luke while I get away long enough to do just that."

"Good." Nash had to remind himself how much Josh and his family meant to Sidney. Maybe it would help Josh if he saw firsthand how happy Sidney usually was. "There's an empty house on the ranch if you're interested. Can't promise you any kind of nightlife, but it's quiet unless the cattle are riled up."

Josh's head tilted to the side. "Thanks. I'll think about it." He glanced at the closed door. "Will you tell him for me?"

"I'll tell him." Nash crossed his arms. "You're a fool if you don't do everything in your power to get him back on your side." He shook his head. "A man couldn't ask for a better friend than Sidney."

"I know," Josh mumbled.

Nash pulled out his wallet and handed Josh one of the Running E's business cards. "There's the address. We won't seek you out again. Next move is yours."

Josh's Adam's apple bobbed up and down several times before he answered. "I understand."

With a final wave, Nash walked back into the room. He sure as hell hoped Josh did understand, because the next time the man hurt Sidney, Nash would deal with the situation his way.

Chapter Twelve

March 1990

Grady Nash was in the process of moving a herd of cattle closer to the house when he spotted Sidney riding towards him at break-neck speed. His immediate reaction was to panic. Cattle forgotten, Nash kicked Rosie into a run.

It wasn't until he came within fifty yards of Sidney that Nash's heart started to beat again. The expression on Sidney's face was one of elation, not pain. Nash pulled Rosie to a stop and waited for Sidney to join him.

"What's going on?" Nash asked.

Sidney reached inside his winter coat and removed a sheet of paper. "I won!"

"Excuse me?" Nash rubbed his chest, trying to settle his racing heart. "What do you mean you won?"

"The contest. The one I told you about. You know, designing the library." Sidney shook the paper in his hand. "I won. They're going to build it. Not only that, but they wanna hire me to oversee the project."

Nash climbed down from his saddle before pulling Sidney off Apple Jack and into his arms. "Congratulations, babe." He gave Sidney a deep kiss. If the cattle hadn't interrupted them, Nash had no doubt he'd have stood there all afternoon tasting his champion.

Nash broke the kiss and glanced over his shoulder at the milling cattle that were beginning to spread out again. "Help me round them back up and get them into the south pasture and I'll help you celebrate."

Nash helped Sidney back onto his horse. He didn't say

it, but he needed a few minutes to process Sidney's news. He truly was happy for Sidney, but he honestly didn't remember enough about the project to know where he was going to have to move.

A thought struck him. "How soon would we need to leave?" he asked, mounting Rosie.

"Relax," Sidney said with a smile. "We don't have to be in Chicago until after graduation."

May? *Fuck.* Nash gripped the reins tighter to keep his hands from shaking. He tried to concentrate on the cattle, but his thoughts began to stray into dangerous territory. Although he'd received his GED, Nash still wasn't sure what kind of job he'd be qualified for in a city like Chicago.

Apple Jack sidled up next to Rosie and Sidney put a hand on Nash's leg. "It'll be okay. I promise."

"Do you think they need mechanics in Chicago? Working on engines is about the only thing I know how to do besides running a ranch."

"I'm sure they probably do, but don't sell yourself short. You've spent the last fifteen years balancing books, figuring payroll, hell, you even know how to type."

Nash let out a snort. "Yeah, I can just see myself being some man's secretary. No thanks. I'd rather do something with my hands."

"Sexist pig. Who says your boss won't be a woman?" Sidney said around a chuckle.

Apple Jack moved away, taking Sidney's warm hand with him. It was a typical move on the horse's part, but it served as a reminder to Nash. He needed that hand. Chicago may not be his idea of the Promised Land, but it sure as hell beat living life without the man he loved.

* * * *

May 1990

Nash pulled at the tie around his neck. He hadn't worn one since his dad's funeral and he was quick to remember why. How the hell men worked in the strangling strip of material, he'd never understand. Deciding he could survive for another few hours, Nash pulled on his suit coat.

It felt strange to be back in the small house he'd rented from Jackson for so many years, but he and Sidney had both agreed to give Tommy the chance to make a go of the ranch. They'd ended up leasing the house and acreage to Tommy with the provision that he'd do general upkeep on the small house on the edge of the Running E in case Sidney and Nash needed a place to return to someday.

"You ready?" Nash asked, walking into the kitchen.

Dressed in a white dress shirt and pair of black pants, Sidney looked up from the graduation card. "Yeah." He held up the cheque that had obviously accompanied the card. "It's from the Ballentines. Maggie says both Luke and Josh have returned to school."

"That's good." Nash opened the fridge and pulled out the gallon of milk. Josh had been in touch with Sidney a few times since their run-in on Thanksgiving. The fence hadn't been completely mended, but Nash could tell Josh was trying, so he kept his mouth shut.

He poured a tall glass of milk and waited for Sidney to finish with the day's mail. "Anything from Jackson?"

Sidney snorted and jumped out of his chair. "You mean you didn't see this?" He grabbed a card off the counter and passed it to Nash.

Nash opened the generic-looking card. Inside Jackson had written, *Good Luck.* "Nice," he said with a shake of his head.

"You can throw it away if you're done with it," Sidney told Nash. "It was so touching I've already committed it to memory."

Although Sidney made light of the situation, Nash knew better. He rinsed out his milk glass before crossing to wrap his arms around the younger man. "Sorry."

Sidney shrugged, but held Nash tighter. "I shouldn't have expected him to come. It was stupid to think he'd make the

161

drive."

Nash pressed his face against Sidney's hair. The smell of citrus clinging to the silky black strands always helped soothe his anger. It was obvious to everyone Jackson's new family had completely replaced Sidney in his life.

According to the gossip Nash had heard at the cattle auction in Salina, Jackson had three children with his wife, two boys and a girl. Not only had Sidney been unaware that he had half-brothers and a half-sister, but the oldest, Jackson Junior, or J.J. as they called him, was around ten. Needless to say, Sidney hadn't taken the news well.

"Fuck him," Nash mumbled. "He'll come crawling back someday begging your forgiveness."

"I won't hold my breath."

Nash glanced at the clock. "If we're going to make it in time for you to walk across that stage, we'd better head out."

Sidney took a step back. "I know you don't really want to sit through this, so thanks for doing it anyway."

"Are you kidding?" Nash leant down until he was nose to nose with Sidney. "Do you think I've been completely blind to how hard you've worked to be able to walk across that stage?" He straightened and gestured to the deep purple graduation robe draped over the back of the chair. "You've earned the right to wear that, and I couldn't be prouder of you."

Sidney tried to smile, but his eyes soon filled with tears. "You've always been there for me. If I had my way, you'd be walking across that damn stage with me."

Nash put his hand over his heart. "I will be."

* * * *

June 1990

On moving day, Nash was up before the sun. He made a pot of coffee, but ended up sneaking his cup under the automatic drip before the full pot was done. Carrying the steaming mug out onto the porch, he sat in a chair and waited.

It was his last day on the ranch he'd grown to love. Later, they'd finish loading the moving truck and drive north to Lake Forest, Illinois. He hoped the small suburb north of Chicago would be a good compromise for the two of them. Sidney would be able to ride the Metra to the city and Nash wouldn't be surrounded by millions of people on a daily basis.

Nash still worried about job prospects for someone like him, but Sidney had assured him he'd find something he could enjoy. Nash sure hoped to hell Sidney was right. Although they had some savings and Sidney would be making decent money to start off, Nash had never been one to let someone else take care of him.

Staring out over the pasture, Nash took a deep, emotional breath when the sun peeked over the horizon. *Glorious.* Some people worshipped God in church, but for Nash, the Running E was the closest he'd ever come to feeling the divine spirit of the man upstairs.

Nash continued to reflect on his life thus far as the sun continued to rise. He'd stepped foot on the Running E almost seventeen years earlier. A young kid who'd lost his dad, looking for a place to heal. Nash chuckled to himself. He'd done more than heal on the ranch over the years. He'd found the man he was meant to be with. Doubts about living away from the ranch might creep into his mind on occasion, but not once did he question his love for Sidney.

Once the orange sun had risen above the horizon, Nash carried his empty cup into the kitchen. He refilled it before getting another cup out of the cupboard for Sidney. Walking into the bedroom, he set the mugs on the bedside table before stripping out of his underwear. Being that it was the last morning of his old life, Nash didn't plan to waste a second of it.

Lifting the covers, Nash slid between the sheets before pressing his body against Sidney's warm back. He hadn't realised how chilly the June morning was until his body came into contact with his little personal furnace. "Mmmm," he moaned, burying his face in Sidney's hair.

Still asleep, Sidney squirmed until his ass was perfectly positioned against Nash's hardening cock.

Nash rested his hand against Sidney's bare chest, lazily brushing his thumb over one of the smaller man's nipples. He closed his eyes and tried to soak in every second. Jesus, he loved the man whose body drove him crazy with lust.

Nash's hand slowly travelled down Sidney's chest to the sparse hair surrounding the younger man's cock. Unlike Nash's pubic hair, Sidney's was as soft as the hair on his head. Nash continued to pet Sidney's groin, loving the way it felt against his fingers.

Two weeks earlier, after signing the rental papers on the house they'd found in Lake Forest, Sidney had asked Nash about getting a dog. When Nash reminded Sidney of his allergies, Sidney had produced a sheet of paper. It was a copy of an article about poodles. Of course Nash knew some dogs were better than others for people with dander allergies, but a poodle? He just couldn't see himself walking a prissy dog around the neighbourhood. He'd promised Sidney they'd discuss it again once they'd moved, knowing full well he'd give in. Sidney must've known it too, because he'd agreed and hadn't spoken of it since.

Nash's brushed his fingertips up and down the length of Sidney's flaccid cock, hoping to wake his lover up without making it obvious. He grinned when Sidney pushed his cock more firmly against Nash's hand.

"If you're trying to wake me up, you'd better give me a little more than that," Sidney mumbled, sleep still heavy in his voice.

Nash encircled Sidney's awakening cock with his hand. "Better?"

"Mmm hmm." Sidney began moving his hips, working his body between Nash's rock hard erection and Nash's hand. "Lube's under my pillow."

"Turn around here and kiss me." As much as Nash wanted to bury his cock in Sidney, he was hoping to make the morning last a little longer. He released Sidney's erection and slapped him on the ass to get him moving.

"Ow!" Sidney protested.

"That didn't hurt, you big baby," Nash chided.

Sidney rolled over and bit Nash's chin.

"Damn!" Nash said with a growl.

"That didn't hurt, you bigger baby," Sidney said around a chuckle.

Nash cut off Sidney's smart mouth with a kiss. He delved deep, hoping to convey his love and desire with each swipe of his tongue.

Sidney moaned and hooked his leg over Nash's hip. He reached under his pillow before shoving the lube into Nash's hand.

Taking the hint, Nash flipped open the bottle and managed to drip a few drops onto his fingers without spilling the contents onto the mattress. He started with the crease of Sidney's ass, running his fingers up and down as he continued to fuck Sidney's mouth with his tongue.

Sidney whimpered into the kiss each time Nash brushed over his hole. God, Nash loved that sound. He purposely continued to tease Sidney just so he could hear it over and over.

Sidney finally reached back and guided two of Nash's fingers to his hole.

Nash broke the kiss. "Maybe I want to hear more whimpers before I give in," Nash complained.

"Fuck me, and I'll whimper like a damn dog in heat."

Giving in, like he usually did, Nash pushed first one then two fingers inside. Sidney's body was so used to Nash's cock, it didn't take long before he was ready.

Sidney reached blindly behind himself and found the bottle of lube. While Nash continued to torment the smaller man with his fingers, Sidney began his own brand of torture by slicking Nash's cock.

A scrape of Sidney's fingernail just under Nash's crown almost made Nash come on the spot. Nash removed his hand from the crease of Sidney's ass before rolling the man onto his stomach.

Nash repositioned Sidney until his knees were underneath him and his ass was in the air. Nash sat back on his heels and licked his lips. Despite hating the taste of lube, he couldn't resist running his tongue over the loosened pucker a few times.

"I'm about two seconds from coming," Sidney said into his pillow.

Nash knew Sidney expected him to stop, but Nash didn't always do what was expected of him. He leant in again and used the tip of his tongue to fuck Sidney.

"Fuck!" Sidney howled. His hole clenched around Nash's tongue as he erupted onto the sheet below.

Before Sidney could collapse, Nash turned him over. He grabbed a pillow and placed it under Sidney's lower back for support. "Okay?"

Still panting from the force of his climax, Sidney nodded. He reached down and held his legs up and apart.

"Is that a suggestion?" Nash chuckled.

Sidney grinned in return. "An order," he managed to get out.

"Ooh, I like it when you take charge." Nash lined his cock up with Sidney's hole. Once past the outer ring of muscles, Nash thrust inside in one smooth move. The heat of Sidney's body drew an immediate groan from Nash.

Maybe making Sidney come before they fucked wasn't such a good idea after all. If Nash had any hope of outlasting Sidney's second orgasm, he'd need to provide Sidney that slight bite of pain he seemed to really enjoy.

Nash began a hard, deep rhythm without giving Sidney time to fully acclimate to the invasion.

Sidney thumped his head back against his pillow. "Ahhh, fuck!"

Satisfied he could get the results he was after; Nash

hooked Sidney's legs over his shoulders to free up his hands. As he continued the assault on Sidney's ass, Nash pinched his lover's pebbled nipples.

"Harder," Sidney screeched.

Nash wasn't sure if Sidney was referring to the fucking or the torture on his nipples, so he decided to give him both. Each thrust slapped Nash's balls against Sidney's smooth ass. The sound of skin on skin, combined with Nash's grunts and Sidney's moans made for an erotic symphony Nash knew he could listen to for the rest of his life.

In the midst of it all, Nash made a mental note to make sure to close the windows before fucking Sidney once they moved to the suburbs. Out in God's country, they could make as much noise as they liked, but unless they wanted to completely alienate their neighbours, they would need to quiet it down once in town. Yet one more reason life in the country was better, in Nash's opinion.

Once Sidney's cock had hardened again, Nash released one of the younger man's nipples. Nash wrapped his hand around Sidney's cock and pressed his thumb against the dripping slit.

Sidney's eyes lit up at the newest sensation.

"Damn, you're beautiful," Nash growled.

Sidney's nostrils flared when Nash slapped his balls.

"You got more of that sweet seed for me?" Nash asked, through gritted teeth. Fuck, he needed to come.

"Yessss," Sidney hissed as the first spurt of cum shot from his cock.

That was all Nash needed to let loose. He shoved his cock as far into Sidney as it would go and came. The orgasm was so intense, Nash's face screwed up as if he was in pain, and in a way, he was.

He collapsed on top of Sidney, afraid he'd never again be able to breathe. Where the hell had that come from? Sure he was getting older, but he was still only thirty-four. He gasped, trying to pull enough oxygen into his lungs to keep from passing out.

"Okay?"

Nash heard the question but was still in no condition to answer so he nodded, hoping to play the incident off. He tried to push the worry out of his mind. It was just a really, really good fuck, he tried to tell himself.

Sidney sucked Nash's earlobe into his mouth before whispering, "The best."

Nash closed his eyes. "Yeah," he managed to say.

* * * *

Sidney stood on the porch with Tommy and his wife, Brynn, while Nash said goodbye to the horses. "Thanks for keeping Rosie," he said. "I know she won't be around too much longer and the thought of her living out her final years on someone else's ranch didn't sit well with Nash."

"She's a good horse," Tommy said.

"Yeah," Sidney agreed. His heart ached for Nash. Not only was he leaving behind the ranch he'd come to love, but they both knew his old truck wouldn't make the ten hour trip. Sidney had suggested using the trailer they were hauling the Bronco on for it, but Nash had declined the offer. He'd said it was time he moved on and bought something else.

Sidney couldn't help but wonder whether it had more to do with the constant reminder of the ranch Nash didn't want to leave. In the end, Nash had sold the pickup to Tommy for his fifteen-year-old son. Sidney had taken Tommy aside and explained to him the significance of the truck to Nash, and Tommy had promised to make sure his son took good care of it.

Nash emerged from the barn, wiping his eyes.

"You driving straight through?" Tommy asked as Brynn disappeared into the house.

"Yep. With luck we'll make it to Lake Forest before midnight," Sidney answered, his eyes never leaving the man walking towards the ranch house. How would he ever be able to repay Nash for the sacrifice he was about to make?

Sidney blinked away the threatening tears as Nash stepped up onto the porch to join him. "How many treats did you give Rosie?" he asked, trying to lift the sadness evident in Nash's face.

It worked. Nash grinned and rested his hand on the small of Sidney's back. "Just enough to make her remember me."

"No worries there. You're pretty damn unforgettable." Sidney moved closer to Nash's side.

The screen door opened and Brynn came out carrying a cooler. "I packed you all a couple of sandwiches, some pop and a few of my homemade oatmeal raisin cookies," she said, handing the cooler to Nash.

Nash tipped his cowboy hat. "Thanks."

Sidney stared at the familiar Stetson. He wondered if Nash would continue to wear it once they started their life together in Chicago.

"Well, we'd better get rollin'." Nash reached out and shook Tommy's hand.

Once Nash had moved on to Brynn, Sidney gave Tommy a hug. "Take care of it."

Tommy nodded. "I will."

Sidney took a step back before turning to Brynn. He didn't know Tommy's wife as well, but gave her a hug anyway. "Take care."

"Be safe," she said, releasing Sidney.

Sidney moved to follow Nash to the rented moving truck. He opened the door, but didn't get in right away. He gave the place one more visual scan.

"Sidney?" Nash prompted, starting the engine.

"Yeah." Sidney glanced up at Nash and smiled. "I hate to admit it, but I'm even gonna miss that damn chicken coop." He climbed up and settled himself in the seat, remembering to put his seatbelt on.

"We'll be back to visit," Nash mumbled.

Sidney could tell Nash was making a concerted effort not to get emotional. "Sure we will," he agreed, reaching over to squeeze Nash's hand. "Thank you."

Nash turned his hand over and threaded his fingers through Sidney's. "Where you go, I go. Always without regrets."

Summer

Excerpt

Chapter One

After sliding into home plate, Grady Nash stood and brushed the dirt off of his pants. The whoops of the small crowd made him feel like a million bucks. He tipped his KC Royals baseball hat to the folks in the bleachers as he walked back to the bench. Trading his beloved cowboy hate for a baseball hat had been tough, but after numerous comments from the guys he worked with, Nash had found it easier to just relent.

"Not bad for an old man," Butch Carlisle said with a slap on the back, nearly knocking Nash to the ground.

"I'm thirty-four," Nash reminded his new friend.

"Yeah, like I said, old." Butch spat a sunflower seed shell on to the ground, the pile growing with each inning of the softball game. Despite his rough appearance, Butch was an okay guy. With shoulders as broad as a barn and forearms the size of Popeye's, Butch's shaved head only added to the biker exterior he liked to cultivate.

Nash crossed his arms and leant back against the dugout's chain link fence. Despite Butch's barbs, Nash felt damn good. He might be older than the others on the team, but he was still young enough to keep up with them.

"We're going to Wally's after the game," Butch said as another shell flew from his mouth.

"Wally's, huh?" Nash tried to remember what time Sidney had said he'd be home. "I could use a beer." Or four. He'd lived in Lake Forest for almost three months and had yet to go out without Sidney, which meant he rarely went out. He'd been lucky one of the guys from the garage hadn't been able to complete the summer softball season or he'd never have left the house that day.

Joe Banks crossed home plate standing up and Nash gave Butch a high five at the come from behind win. Nash followed the rest of the players out of the dugout to acknowledge the effort of the opposing team with hand slaps.

He returned to the bench and picked up his glove. Unlike the other players on the team, Nash didn't own any equipment besides the old beat-up glove he'd used in high school. "I'll follow you," he told Butch as they headed to the parking lot.

Nash climbed into his red Ford pickup. He'd need to call home as soon as he got to the bar. Was it a bad thing that he secretly hoped Sidney was still at the job site? It wasn't that he didn't love Sidney's company, but he was ready to make a few friends of his own. The guys at the garage, where he'd finally found a job, had been pretty good about welcoming him, but Nash wanted more than that. He'd got used to life on the ranch where camaraderie seemed to come naturally. It wasn't that he was looking for a new best friend—Sidney would forever hold that position in his life—but he enjoyed watching the men at the garage laugh and tease each other.

More books from
Carol Lynne

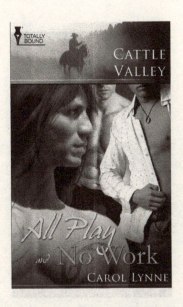

Book one in the bestselling Cattle Valley series
It's time to head for greener pastures.

Carol Lynne

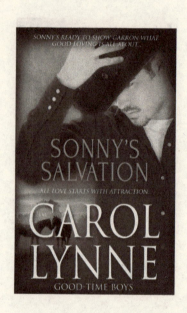

Book one in the Good-time Boys series

*An openly gay rancher in the middle of Nebraska just
doesn't have many prospective dates.*

About the Author

Carol Lynne

An avid reader for years, one day Carol Lynne decided to write her own brand of erotic romance. Carol juggles between being a full-time mother and a full-time writer. These days, you can usually find Carol either cleaning jelly out of the carpet or nestled in her favourite chair writing steamy love scenes.

Carol Lynne loves to hear from readers. You can find contact information, website details and an author profile page at https://www.pride-publishing.com/

PRIDE PUBLISHING